Our Maureen

Adventures of a Lincolnshire Lass

Maureen Bakelmun

PublishAmerica
Baltimore

ISBN: 1-60563-862-5
PUBLISHED BY PUBLISHAMERICA, LLLP
www.publishamerica.com
Baltimore

Printed in the United States of America

Dedication

To Morgan, Alister and Levon

Acknowledgments

I want to thank Helen and Errol Thornton for all their assistance. Even with a broken shoulder Helen was always there to help this semi-computer-literate computer operator. Without her the tale would have been floating about in the ether.

Wendy Tchir, you were always an encouragement to me; it was with your prompting that the book was written.

I have been blessed to have many faithful friends all over the world, some of whom are in these stories. I always thank God for you all.

Table of Contents

Part 1
A Scunthorpe Childhood

The Ironing Board Incident

It was a rainy summer day. We kids were on school holidays, so Audrey, my friend who lived up the street, and I decided to play indoors with our dolls. We were still at the doll age of about 10 or 11 years old. My mam was at work, so we had the house to ourselves. I had a little black terrier dog, Cheater, named after the monkey in the Tarzan movies. Well, Audrey was deathly afraid of dogs; actually she was afraid of lots of things. She was, in fact, quite a jittery.

We went into the front room to play. We left my dog Cheater in the kitchen with the door firmly closed. When we got the dolls out we saw that all their clothes were crumpled. So we decided that we should iron them, like the proper little mothers we thought we were. I had seen my mam do the ironing lots of times. She would never let me help her with the ironing no matter how much I pleaded. I could never understand why; I knew I could do it. So I got the iron out.

Now we did not have an ironing board. My mam would use the kitchen table, but we were not in the kitchen, and the dog was. So we put the ironing cloth on the dining table. I don't know why, but the plug on the end of the iron had an attachment for the light socket. I guess in the *olden days* electricity was only for lights. I can't remember any wall sockets if there were any at all. So up on the table I got, unplugged the light, and plugged in the iron. We did not know how long the iron would take to heat up. So me in my wisdom suggested that we go into the kitchen, and I would teach Audrey how not to be afraid of our dog. Even at that age I was such a smart aleck.

We were playing in the kitchen for some time, forgetting about the dolls and the iron. Audrey took a sniff and said, "Can you smell smoke?"

I sniffed. No, I couldn't.

Once again we were engrossed with the dog. My little Cheater was such a lovely little dog. She was all black, and I'm sure she had some Jack Russell in her; she was very active and loved to go hunting rabbits. That would eventually cause her demise. Then once again Audrey, with a scared look in her eyes, said, "I can smell burning!" Now I took a good long hard sniff. Yes, there was burning, *somewhere*. Then we both looked at each other. If Audrey's face was anything like mine, then I must have looked terrified. THE IRON! We both ran into the other room. Oh! My goodness. Silly, silly, silly me! I had left the iron face down on the table. What a sight met us as we opened the door.

The room was full of smoke. The iron had burnt through the ironing cloth and through the table top. The iron was hanging by its cord, almost pulling the light fixture out of the ceiling. It was now burning through the table legs. Well, we both went into panic mode. I didn't have the sense to turn off the light at the wall. Instead I picked up the iron, and then just like the silly 10-year-old that I was, I put it down again, *face down*. The iron was red hot by now, so of course you know what happened. It started to burn another hole in the table.

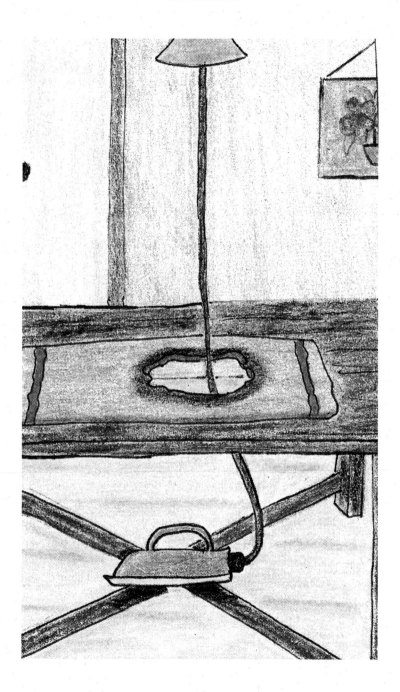

Audrey had a little more sense than me. She ran into the kitchen, forgetting her fear of the dog, got a cup of water, and threw it onto the scorching mess. That didn't do much good. It just created a lot of steam, but it was a good effort. I at last turned the light off at the wall. When I turned around I just caught the back of Audrey as she hightailed it out of the house. It was like watching a cartoon character in slow motion. I saw her as she was running up the street, flailing her arms about in a real panic, crying, "Oh my, oh my!"

Then as providence would have it, my mam was coming down the road on her bike. She saw Audrey running up the street like she was on fire. When Audrey saw my mam she was still flailing her arms about, doing little hopping steps, just as if she was on fire. "Oooh, oooh, Mrs Hill, your Maureen has set your house on fire!"

Well, you can imagine my mam's reaction. She must have thought there would be a burning heap where her home used to be. So I think when she saw that it was only her *best* dining table, and the room full of smoke, I believe she was almost relieved. I didn't get a hiding for that one, which was a surprise to me.

The insurance covered the cost of having the table refinished and repaired. When it was returned it was as good as new, so all was well.

It is only years later that I realised that Audrey was never allowed to play with me any more.

I wonder why?

The Monkey Tree

I was about twelve years old and had not a care in the world. Life was just for fun and adventure. My friends were the same age as I and just as carefree.

School was out for the summer. My friends Kathleen, Theresa, and I were wondering what we could do. It was a nice warm day, and after months of being in the classroom we just wanted to be outside in the sunshine. At the bottom of my street there was a wooded area. That's where we were headed this day. We were not sure what we were going to do, but fun and adventure was on the menu.

In this wood there was a huge old tree. As kids would do we had to give it a name. So we called it the Monkey Tree. I am sure there are kids all over the world that have a Monkey Tree somewhere in their adventures. This tree was so old that there were barely any leaves on it. Some of the local lads had climbed to the top and tied a good thick rope onto the topmost branch. A stick tied to the other end of the rope made an ideal swing. So we three decided that we would have some fun. We were just as adventurous as the boys. We would stand on the branch of another tree and swing through the air. Oh, boy, it would be fun! We would be just like Tarzan in the movies. We picked out a tree with a good strong branch sticking out about 8 feet off the ground. How we decided who should go first I cannot remember, but Kathleen was the first to go. She was the smallest and the most daring. She climbed up the tree and out onto the branch. We threw the end of the rope up to her. She wasted no time, Stuck the stick seat between her legs, grabbed hold of the rope, and jumped, swinging through the air like a trapeze flyer. With a whoop and holler she swung back and forth, having a wonderful time.

It looked like so much fun I could hardly wait for my turn; I was the next one to go. I was looking forward to the swing through the air. Kathleen jumped off the rope. Now was my turn. Oh, no! Theresa was trying to sneak up the tree before me. If only I had been more gracious and let her go ahead. Oh, no, not I; instead I grabbed her and pulled her down, saying, "Oh, no you don't; it's my turn next."

She gave in and let me climb up the tree, out onto the branch. Anticipation was running high. Someone passed the rope up to me; I grabbed it and put the stick seat between my legs, and thought I was going to have the highest swing ever. I was going to be free, free, free like a bird. I took a deep breath and jumped as high as I could. If I did not have to hold on to the rope I would have beaten my chest just as Tarzan would have done in one of his movies. Shouting the Tarzan shout, Aah-oo-ah!" I swung off the branch just as free as a bird. I could feel the wind blowing through my hair and my dress billowing out behind me. I felt that I could do almost anything. That feeling did not last for long, in the back of my mind I heard a snap. Then I realised it was the rope; there was nothing I could do. I was plummeting to the ground. It was a horrible feeling, and I could do nothing to stop the fall.

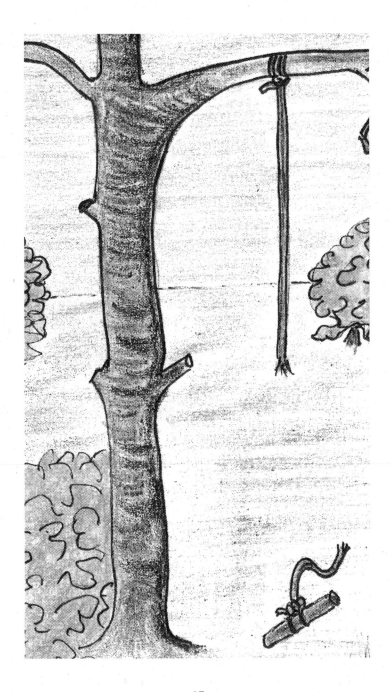

After that everything happened so quickly. I came crashing to the ground. I was stunned for quite a while. I still had the rope clasped in my hands, as if that would save me. I had the wind well and truly knocked out of me. Gasping for breath I thought I would never be able to breathe again. I could feel panic rising in me. When I finally could breathe I tried to move, but the pain was really searing. Not only my backside, but everywhere hurt. Then I realised why all the pain. Not only had I hurt myself falling, I had fallen into the middle of a large bramble bush. This, thankfully, had broken my fall, but now the thorns were pricking me all over. I was still hurting pretty badly, and when I tried to move not only did my back hurt, but even at the slightest movement the thorns on the bramble bush pricked and scratched me. I was laughing and crying at the same time. Even though I hurt I could see the funny side of the situation. I was in a real predicament. The bramble bush was so dense it had broken my fall, thank goodness, but now I could not get out. I was trapped in a thorny prison. The other two were not much help. Even though they knew I must have hurt myself they couldn't help laughing, as it really was a funny situation. Even cartoon like, I half expected the road runner to go speeding past, beep beeping. There I was, stuck in the middle of a bramble bush, and no way for them to get in or me to get out.

A lady had been walking down Crosby Road Hill, and she had seen the whole thing from the road. She was really worried and came running into the wood, shouting, "Oh, my goodness, you silly girls! Oh, you silly girls! You could have been killed!"

She was probably right, but I didn't need to hear that at this time. She could see the predicament I was in, and she quickly went into action. She took off her coat; because of the uncertainty of the weather in England everyone wore a coat. She threw her coat onto the bramble bush, and then ordered my mates to help her stomp on it to flatten out the branches. Then she reached me and helped me up, and made sure nothing was broken. She then told my friends to help me home. Well, I needed help, I can tell you, I could only take little slow steps. Even the fabled tortoise could have raced me and won.

It took us ages to get home. It wasn't very far, not even two blocks, but it took me about half an hour to reach my house. I had to stop every few yards because of the pain.

Kathleen went running on ahead to tell my mam what had happened; my mother was used to me getting into scrapes, bumps, and scratches, so she made very light of it. My friends thought my mam was a mean old thing, until that evening. I was still moaning and groaning whenever I moved.

She said, "Let's have a look at your back, our Maureen." When she saw the huge black, blue, and purple bruise she said, "Oh my, Oh my!" and I am sure felt very sorry that she had taken no notice earlier. She immediately ran a hot bath for me to soak in. That felt nice and soothing. Then she rubbed on some ointment. I don't know what good it did, but I felt like I was getting much needed attention. I had a little respite for a day or two, but soon everything was back to normal. I still managed to have a summer full of adventures.

Years later I still have problems with my back. I should think it is from that fall.

The Fun of Pole Vaulting

I was very fortunate as a child. I had a safe and happy childhood; I was born and raised in Scunthorpe; a town in Lincolnshire, England. Now Scunthorpe was a steel industrial town. History has it that a lord had come to the manor house to do some hunting, and while out in the fields he tripped over a rock. This rock had iron in it, and as there were a lot of these rocks it was deemed profitable to mine it. I'm sure it was profitable for the lord of the manor. Anyway, that's how Scunthorpe became a steel industrial town. Most of the men in town either worked on the steel works or in related industry. It was interesting to see the workmen coming and going to work as the shift changed. Cars were a novelty and only for the rich. All the rest had bikes; it was like a sea of bikes coming and going up and down the high street. It was a real rush hour. Years later I saw a documentary about China with all the bikes on the road. That was what it was like in my home town when I was a child.

I had a really happy-go-lucky childhood with no worries, no cares. I used to have so much fun when I was a child. I was the only girl down my street; therefore, I had to be pretty tough.

One summer day Gordon, who lived across the street, and I went to play down the road on Atkinson's Warren. All us kids called it Ackie's Warren. It was a huge tract of land. It must have been acres and acres of land. Part of it was the warren. That was on the hill and had some pretty amazing sand pits. In the winter we would go sledding down there. Along the top of the sand pits there was this very dense wood full of old, large trees. There was one tree that had four trunks. We called it our lucky tree and would imagine if we sat under it we would have some wonderful adventure. It never happened. But that didn't stop us from dreaming.

The other way, down the sand pits at the bottom of the hill, there was a rough cart track. Cross that track, and you were in the bottom wood. This wood was full of young trees and lots of bushes. There were quite a few animals; rabbits, foxes, and pheasants all lived in this wood. If truth be known, my dad would go poaching there just after the war, World War II, when everything was on ration. This was one way of boosting our protein and stretching our rations.

This was where we were going today, but first we would take another ramble down this cart track past the Atkinson's farm house. It was a beautiful day. The sun was warm on our faces. A bit farther down this track there was a ruin of an old, old church. Now when I say old, I mean really old. There was very little of the church left, just part of two broken-down walls.

We had vivid imaginations and would think that we could find some treasure. We would mooch around there, kicking stones and poking about. Little did we realize that the treasure was there all the time. There were gravestones marred by age, some tilting over, some completely fallen down. The ravages of time had taken its toll. Some of them could not be read at all, but there were a couple we were just able to read. They dated back to the late 1600s. I went back years later and was shocked to see that the slag from the steel works had covered this wonderful old treasure completely. England is so full of old buildings that this one will not be missed, except by me.

Well, on this day Gordon and I were going to have some fun in the woods. We ambled back the couple of miles down the track, retracing our steps. There was a creek running through the wood that was so overgrown with grass that the bank of the creek was hidden. I stepped on what I thought was the edge of the creek, and splash! In I went. It was not very deep, so I only wet my shoes and socks; my white socks were not white any more. I didn't even think of what my mother would say. She took a lot of pride keeping her family clean. That was the farthest thing from my mind on this beautiful day. After Gordon stopped laughing at my predicament, he suggested that we find some good strong poles. Then we could pole vault over the stream. Well, that was the best way over, or so we thought. We didn't look to see if there was another way over. We were in the woods, so it was not too difficult to find two good strong poles. We got a couple about 5 feet long. That would do.

Gordon, being the boy, thought he should go first and show me how it was done. The creek was only a few feet wide, three feet at the most. We were sure we could leap this bit of water, no problem. What did we know? We were just kids. Anyway, he took a bit of a run at it, stuck his pole in the water, and leaped, his legs making a running motion in midair. Well! He missed the bank, landing good and square in water covering his ankles. Now it was my turn to have a good laugh.

Eventually we did manage to leap across the stream. We played for like what seemed hours. Then our tummies gave us notice that it was time to return home to some good homemade bread and homemade jam. We took our poles along with us. They were proof that we had mastered the art of pole jumping. Dragging our poles we trudged up the warren, which seemed a lot steeper now. We had played ourselves out. Walking up our street we must have looked a pretty sorry sight. We were all muddy, wet, and disheveled, dragging our poles as if they weighed a ton. No one gave us a second look because we looked that way more often than not during the school holidays. When I got home my mother had done the washing, so I guess that must have been a Monday. She was now hanging the clothes on the line. The warm summer breeze would dry them in no time.

When she saw me and the mess I was in she asked, "What on earth have you been up to, our Maureen?"

Well, that was all I needed to relate the adventures that Gordon and I had.

My Mother asked, "And what on earth are you doing with that blooming big stick?"

"Oh, mam!" I said, "This is not a stick; it's a pole for pole vaulting over streams!" Then I proceeded to give her an exhibition of how we jumped over the stream. I took a deep breath, stuck my tongue out in concentration, and took a big run with my pole. I stuck the pole into the ground not thinking of anything but my jump to impress my mam. Wow, it was going to be the best jump ever! Up into the air I flew. Then with a loud thud everything went wrong. The top of the pole hit the clothesline. My chin hit the pole, with my tongue still lolling out of my mouth, and then the searing pain hit me. The pole fell, I fell, and I put my hand to my mouth and shouted, "Mam, Mam!"

My mam, well used to my antics, said, "Oh, now what is it?" rather impatiently, I thought.

I took my hand from my mouth to show her where I was hurting. She let out a blood-curdling scream. It surprised me so much that I'm sure my eyes bulged out of my head. The way she yelled I thought I must have knocked out all my teeth or something. It certainly felt like it. I looked at my hand and was shocked to see it was full of blood. No wonder my mam had screamed. It looked like I had bitten my tongue off.

That was all I needed. I started to cry and howl. That did not make matters any better. For a second or two it was like bedlam. Then at that opportune moment my mam's boss drove up in his car. As I said earlier, not many people had cars in those days in merry old England, so this was a stroke of good luck. That was just what we needed. He saw the situation and quickly went into action. Mam grabbed one of her newly washed towels, put it to my mouth, and the next thing I knew we were at Scunthorpe General Hospital. I don't know why but it was never just "the hospital." Everyone used the full name when they talked about it. It was a new hospital; that could be why. Everyone was proud of the new Scunthorpe Hospital.

Once at the hospital we were rushed into a side room where I was given a painkiller. If you have never had an injection in your tongue I would not recommend it. I don't understand why nowadays young people go and get their tongues pierced. I didn't realize how sensitive the tongue really is. The doctor said to be brave. I didn't feel the necessity to be brave; I was in hospital having a needle stuck into my tongue. A very nice nurse held my hand while the injection took effect. Then an amused doctor proceeded to take out this huge, curved needle. While he made remarks such as "I have never seen anyone who has bitten their own tongue before," I thought, *What a silly thing to say!* I wondered who would go around biting someone else's tongue. Then he proceeded to stick the thing into my mouth.

This was when I realised the injection hadn't taken. I could feel the whole flipping thing. I could feel the needle piercing the skin and being pulled out, and the cat gut being pulled through my flesh. They all said I was very brave, and I'm sure I was. That was when the doctor said that the injection sometimes does not work very well on the tongue. He went on to explain about nerve endings and stuff like that. That didn't make any difference to me; it hurt, and hurt a lot. And yes, I was brave. If I played my cards right I could make the most of this, getting a lot of sympathy and attention.

We went home, I with a piece of cat gut and two stitches in my mouth. Eating was a bit of a problem, but you can bet I didn't starve. That bread and jam still sounded good to me. The doctor had said that the stitches would just dissolve and that I would not have to return to the hospital. Well, the stitches did fall out, but the wound did not knit together. So until this day I have a scar on my tongue. It is quite easy to see where the teeth penetrated.

When I see these young kids today having rings put in their tongues I tell them to beware, as I had one years ago and it didn't work, saying I have the scar to this day. They laugh until I show them the scar. I don't think it has deterred anyone from having hole poked into their body. Still, I try.

When I returned to school after the holidays I was the center of attraction for a few days. If anyone asked I would stick out my tongue to all the aahs and oohs. I was quite the hero for a few days.

The Doncaster Trip

I looked forward to my summer and all that was in store for me. I realise now what a carefree childhood I had. I just knew that I would have a good summer.

Tony Bones, my cousin who was one year older than me, said that we should go for a bike ride. He said we could go to Doncaster. "It's not very far." He was older than I, so must know what he was talking about.

"Oh! Good," I said, "we can go to see my Grandma Hill." So off we tootled to my house to ask my mam if we could have a bottle of pop and some sandwiches. Naturally she wanted to know why. We told her we were going to Grandma Hill's house.

"Oh, no you're not," she said.

We did not realize how far it was to Doncaster from Scunthorpe. So we thought quickly and asked if we could have some sandwiches and drinks anyway. Now my mam was no dummy; she could guess what was in our minds. She said we could have a bottle of water only. We said, "Okay." That was better than nothing.

Mam wanted to know where we were going.

We told her we would go to the River Trent, which was only a couple of miles away.

"Okay," she said, "and don't get into any mischief." Mam stood on the top step and watched as we went on our way. I'm sure she was making sure we went in the direction of the river. My mother told me afterwards she was confident I would not go to Doncaster, as I had on an old gingham dress that I had torn on one of my adventures and had attempted to sew it myself. It was all scrunched up and looked a mess. She failed to take into consideration that as yet I had not grown up enough to be concerned with my appearance. It was much more important for me to have fun.

When Tony and I got to the river he said, "You know Doncaster is not very far. Do you think we should go there anyway?" Now remember, he was one year older, so was pretty smart, or so I thought. I could trust his judgment, and I was game for anything. So off we went along Scoter Bottom. When we got to the Barclay Hotel we turned west on to the A-25, the Scunthorpe-to-Doncaster Road.

I have since found out that the trip to Doncaster is 25 miles, and that's just one way. Once there we would have to come back. We didn't even think about how long it would take us. We left Scunthorpe at about 1 o clock. There were lots of things for us kids to see on the way. There is a canal running alongside the road. So we stopped for a while, threw some rocks into the water, paddled about a bit, had a drink of water, then on our way again. This was a busy road, Lorries [trucks] and buses zoomed past us. We were not at all perturbed; we were, after all, on our adventure. We got to the turn off for the village of Crowl. Tony said we were almost there. What did he know? He was only thirteen. I knew no better, and so I believed him. In actual fact it is only about one quarter of the way there. Believing we were almost there we had another swig of water, and with renewed vigour were on our way. We rode past several farms on the way, with cows and horses, all with their unmistakable smells. That was enough for us to peddle even faster and get away from the pong.

Another seven or eight miles later we came to a T-junction in the road. Now did we turn left or right? Tony again made the executive decision to turn left. It is a good job he did, because had we turned right we would have ended up in Goole, a town in the opposite direction to Doncaster, going towards Leeds. Had we gone that way we would have been well and truly lost. By this time we were getting quite weary and could have turned back. But a little further along the road we saw the sign that announced, DONCASTER. We knew we were at the doorstep, so to speak. Our pedaling got a little more vigorous. In reality we had about eight more miles to go. Then, in what seemed like an age, we were at the main junction for Doncaster.

The surrounding countryside was now familiar to me. I had been to Doncaster many times with my mam and dad and knew we had to turn to the right to get to Grandma's house. To the left out of the corner of my eye I saw this big sign that read, LONDON A-1. I said to Tony, "Look! We are almost at London! It's only one mile. Shall we go there?"

He thought for a while then said, "Oh, I don't know, Maureen. I think it is farther than that."

What silly kids we were, not realising that A-1 was the name of the main trunk road to London. In reality London was about 130 miles farther on. I dread to think what would have happened to us had we gone that way. And we were getting rather hungry. Grandma did make some good food. She always had treats that no one else did. Even during the war, that's World War II, when things were on ration, she always managed to get black-market stuff. I can remember her having tins of tuna and tins of mandarin oranges. She also acquired many foods that I had never eaten before, so common sense and our growling tummies took over, and we turned to the right.

We had to go right through the center of town. Now Doncaster is usually quite a busy town. But today the traffic seemed particularly heavy. There were cars, lorries, buses, even horse trailers all rushing through town. We thought it was because it was Saturday and a shopping day. We were wrong again. It seemed like we were wrong most of the time. This Saturday was in fact, "Derby Day." That is the day that they have the horse race by the same name right there in Doncaster. Racing people from all over the country came to Doncaster to see the races. So that's why the traffic was so heavy, with horse trailers and all.

I knew we were getting close to Grandma's house when we crossed the River Don. Of course we had to stop and have a look at it. It was a good excuse to stop and take a rest. This was at a time when no one thought of pollution. The factories along the river had spilled out their toxic waste, polluting the river. As the river rushed along bubbles foamed, and to us it was quite amazing to see all this froth and foam. In reality, if anyone had fallen into the water you would never have found them. There was about four or five feet of foam and froth, and it had a pinkish hue to it. If the foam didn't get them, then the pollution would.

On we went, finally coming to the bridge crossing the railway junction. All the train tracks were running under the bridge. These trains carried passengers north to Scotland and south to London. There were some train spotters taking down the numbers of the trains. I could never understand how they could stand for hours just to get some silly numbers. I don't know what is so interesting about that, but a lot of people do go train spotting, mostly lads, so it must have its attraction.

Now I knew that at last we were almost there. I knew this because when I stayed at my grandma's house she put me in the little front bedroom. The trains would lull me to sleep at night and wake me up in the mornings with their tooting horns and the clackety clack as they ran down the tracks: such happy memories of my childhood. Even now the sound of trains reminds me of Grandma Hill's house.

I saw the road sign, SPROTBROUGH ROAD. We were here. Now we had to turn left and cross the main A-1 to get onto Sprotbrough Road. As I think about it now it was really a very dangerous situation. Cars zoomed north out of town and others zoomed into town and south in the direction of London. We had to dodge between them, but by the grace of God we made it in one piece. Now we were at Grandma's house. Only now did we wonder or even consider, what if Grandma was not home? Dumb kids, we never thought ahead. Hoping and praying that Grandma was home we went up the garden path to the back door. In our part of the country we did not even think of going to the front door. The front door was only for emergencies. I recall a time or two when someone came to the front door, and the apprehension that was felt by everyone. We opened the back door, and there was grandma working in her kitchen. She was a very industrious woman. She would sew and knit; she always had some piece of work in her hands. The family used to boast that one day she looked in a shop window at a Fair Isle Pullover. (That's a sleeveless sweater–a vest.) She looked at it for about half an hour, then she went to the local wool shop, bought the wool, and knitted the pullover without a pattern, just from memory. Quite a feat, as there were 14 different-coloured wools and designs patterns. Nothing could deter her from her objectives. The pullover was for my dad, and to my eyes it was a work of art. I also remember how amazed the family was when, at the age of seventy, she said she had read about slip covers for furniture. Well, she bought the material and made covers for her furniture.

When she saw me she said, "Hello, luv." Then she looked around and said, "Where's your mam?" When we proudly told her what we were on our own she nearly flipped. "All that way? On your bikes? And you came through town? Oh, my goodness, you came today of all days!" Now being a betting woman she knew what day it was and how heavy the traffic was. I'm sure she even had a pound or two on the races herself. "Oh, my goodness!" she said. "Anything could have happened to you! Does your mam know you have come?"

Well, we had to say, no. Grandma would have thought she was a pretty poor mam had she allowed us to come all this way alone on our bikes.

Now at that time in England telephones were at a premium. Not every one could get one. My grandma certainly did not have one. If you were rich, which we were not, or if you had connections, and we did not, or even a situation where you had to get a doctor in an emergency, something like that, then with some wrangling you could get a phone. There was a family down our street that had a daughter who was mentally challenged and had fits; now they had a phone. Grandma could not make a phone call to anyone. Quickly she made us some tea, which was a real treat. She had homemade scones, ham, and some of those mandarin oranges. As I said, Grandma was a good cook. Good plain English cooking. By the time we had eaten it was about 6 o'clock in the evening. Because it was summertime it was still light and would stay light for another three or four hours.

Grandma gave us half a crown each, that's two shillings and six pence, and sent us on our way. We stopped at a goodie or sweet shop just outside Doncaster, bought ourselves some candies, and pop, then we were on our way. We were not looking forward to the trip home with the same anticipation as the trip there. If truth be known we were both rather tired, but we slogged on like troupers. We had no choice; we had to get home. When I think back, Grandma must have been in a state, worrying if we would get home safe and sound.

Being a kid you don't think beyond the moment. We arrived back home at about 9 p.m. Now it was almost dark, and only now did I wonder what my mam would say. I would probably get a good beating. So we went to Tony's house first. It was only a few streets from my house. Aunt Molly would know what to do. She would certainly not beat us. She was in a flap, saying that my mam and dad were worried silly. She made Tony come home with me and maybe break the ice a bit. Then I could possibly avoid a good hiding. We rode our bikes down the street, wondering what my fate would be as we got closer to my house. My mother was standing on the doorstep with Aunt Lil from across the road. Aunt Lil was always in on everything. She was not really an aunt but had been a family friend for donkey's years. So in respect, we called her "aunt."

When they saw these two bedraggled, weary kids riding down the road my mam shouted to my dad, "Frank! Frank! They are here."

I was surprised there was no anger, just relief. Hugs and kisses and tears of relief. That meant no beating. It was now after 9 o'clock at night. My dad was supposed to be on night shift that started at 10 o'clock. Mam said that she wouldn't let him go to work until I came home. I'm sure he needed no prompting. They sent Tony home, then turned to me. They of course wanted to know where we had been. When I told them that we had been to Grandma Hill's I could see a spark in my mam's eyes, but then she said, "Oh my! Our Maureen. What must your grandma be thinking?" Even to this day I don't know how they let Grandma know we were home safe.

I had some more supper, then a hot bath, then off to bed to get rested up for another day. It was, after all, summer holidays, so I had to cram in as much as possible before returning to school.

Little Steven

This story, I think, will be the hardest of all to tell. I lived on a council estate in the small Lincolnshire town of Scunthorpe, in England. My house was a semi-detached house. In the house facing our back door lived a family called the Rileys. Mrs Riley was not the best-liked person on the street. The kids were my friends. They were all more or less the same age as I was. There was Joan, the eldest, a little older than I, and then came Danny, who was my age. We played together a lot. I was a bit of a tough kid. When we played I would punch him or push him. His response was always "Oh! My bad arm!" or, "Oh, my bad leg!" I remember thinking, *Poor Danny; he hurts everywhere.* Eventually I realised he really did not hurt; it was just his way of not letting me win. Once we had made a home phone with two tin cans and a length of string. One end was in his bedroom window, one in mine. It didn't work very well, but that did not matter; we could talk to each other through the open windows anyway.

Terry was one year younger than Danny. Bobby one year younger still, and then came little Steven, who was three years old. I remember Steven when he was little more than a baby. I would put him in my doll's pram and wheel him up and down the yard. He was just like a living doll to me. As he got older he would come and stand at the fence between our houses and call to my mother, shouting "Mrs Hill, can I have some jam tarts?" He was just the sweetest little blond boy.

Now as I said, Mrs Riley was not the best-liked person on the street. Friends were coming and going at all times. In the end my mam had a high fence put up to keep out the view of all the comings and goings, as my mam would say all the "carrying on." The straw that

33

broke the camel's back was when Mrs Riley and a friend were having a big row; he was so mad he picked up the first thing that was close at hand, which was the iron. He bashed her upside of her head. She had stitches and a stay in the hospital for that one. She had a steady man friend for about 4 years. He was the father of Steven. He was more respectable than any of the other friends, but Mrs Riley got tired of him and eventually and kicked him out. He had tried to get custody of Steven, but in those days custody was always given to the mother no matter how dubious or questionable her character. The father of Steven had got a job out of town.

He came to the house to tell Mrs Riley that he wanted to say goodbye to Steven, as he was going away. Not suspecting anything, she said okay. He went up to the bedroom. One bed was shared by all the boys. He came down the stairs and out the door so quickly that Mrs Riley told Danny to go check up on our Steven. This is where my recollection of that night's events begins.

It was one of those warm balmy summer evenings when you had to have all the windows open to get some fresh air. As I said, our house sided up to their house, so our landing window faced their landing window. I was in bed and just falling asleep when I heard the most awful, blood-curdling scream, then a rapid bang, bang, bang, as someone ran downstairs. It was almost like they were falling down the stairs. The next thing I remember was Danny standing at the bottom of our stairs crying, "Oh, Maureen, he has killed our Steven."

My heart still wrenches as I think about it. I wanted to run downstairs and just hug him. Instead I just stood at the top of the stairs, not able to move, partly because I was in my nightgown and was embarrassed. And I was just so stunned. The rest of that evening was just a big blur. I got dressed and went downstairs. It seems that all at once our house was filled with activity. Mam made me help a little. Then she decided that I should go back upstairs. I couldn't understand why at the time, but once I got the whole story I understood.

I found out that Steven's father had gone upstairs with the intention of saying goodbye to his son, but had, in fact, killed him. Danny went up to check on his little brother. The horrific sight that met him must have put him into a state of shock. He saw his brother Steven in bed with the other two boys with his throat cut. His head had been almost severed. The other two sleeping children, Terry and Bobby, were covered in his blood. It was a blessing that they had not awakened to see the sight.

I am sure that the police were called, although I can't remember seeing them at the house. My mother moved into action. She brought the children in to our home. It was her job to clean the blood off them. She scrounged clothing from the neighbours, so that the poor little ones would have clean clothes to wear.

They were not very well cared for, and all were in need of a good hot bath. Aunt Lil came to help. She and my mam were always helping each other. I only realised years later what awful trauma my mam went through. The children were all welcomed in the house. The mother was not. My mam refused to let her into the house. That was something that I just could not understand, how my mother, who was usually so compassionate, could be so heartless. She was, after all, the boy's mother. It was her child that had been brutally slaughtered. That was something that I had to prayerfully deal with in later years. There she was, in a daze sitting on our backdoor step. She looked a pathetic sight. My heart went out to her.

It seemed to me that the next few months went quietly by. I never saw Danny or any of the children again, and I really missed them. I always thought that they would come back. Only when new people moved into their house did I realise that they would not be coming back. The new people were very nice, but it was not the same. My friends were all gone, and I missed them all, even Mrs Riley.

The time soon came around for the trial. The trial was not held in Scunthorpe but at the Lincoln assizes. Lincoln is about thirty miles from our home town. My mam and dad had to go to testify. They had to go several days. Steven's father pleaded guilty. He said that he had tried to get legal custody, but had been denied, and that he would rather

Steven was dead than living in that household in that kind of moral environment. They gave him a very lenient life sentence. I believe he spent 12 years in jail, getting out with good behaviour. At that time that was quite a liberal sentence. I believe the judge had pity on the father after hearing the character of the mother. After the ordeal of the trial my mother came home and collapsed. The doctor said it was delayed shock. It took her a while to get over that one.

Eventually my mother bounced back. What do they say? "You can't keep a good woman down," and my mam was a good woman.

I never saw any of the Riley children again, even though they still lived in the same town. Probably that was for the best. It would have only brought back painful memories for us all. I heard years later that Mrs Riley suffered from severe crippling arthritis and that her children all lovingly took care of her. I understand that she later said what a fool she had been, because Mrs Hill would have been a good neighbour if she had only let her.

A Family Matter

This is not a happy memory. It is however something that happened to my family, and I think the story should be told.

I must have been about 9 or 10 years old when this all took place. My mother, Mildred, had three brothers, Allen, Fred, and Bert. Bert was the eldest. Now when he started work at age 14, he went to work on the steel works in my home town, Scunthorpe, in Lincolnshire, England. On his first day at work he was in an accident and lost one of his legs. This was a very traumatic thing to happen to such a young lad. The company treated him very well, and when he recovered there was always a job for him on the Frodingham steel works. My mother says that because of the accident my grandmother favoured him, and he was spoiled. It could have also been that he was born out of wedlock, a love child, so to speak. That is just a little bit of the background of my uncle Bert.

Uncle Bert had five children. There was Bert the eldest, then came Alfred, Margaret, Mildred, and Maureen. They all lived just a few streets from us. Uncle Bert had a live-in "house keeper," Lilly, and their little girl Mary. All lived together in the three-bedroom house. Lilly had a son 15 years old by a former marriage. This boy was living with his aunty.

It was autumn time, quite cold and damp, when these fateful events took place. This young boy was no longer able to stay with his aunt. He came to his mother at Uncle Bert's and asked if he could stay there, as he had nowhere else to go. Uncle Bert said a definite no. Apparently Lilly cried and pleaded with Bert. Still the answer was a resounding no. She had to send her son out into the cold, to who knows what fate. I am sure this just broke her heart. She was very distraught. She prepared the evening meal for Bert and his family. She must have felt like an unpaid servant. Then, in what must have been an awful state of distress, she said goodbye to Bert and kissed her little girl, saying she was going out.

Now why Uncle Bert didn't ask where she was going or even try to stop her I don't know. He was fed; that was all that counted to him. She then went out into the cold, rainy night. She walked two miles to the River Trent. I can only imagine her state of mind on that fateful night as she threw herself into the dark, cold waters of the river. They found her body the next morning. On the river bank was a scribbled note in her handbag, saying she could no longer live in such a fashion, no hope of anything better. The thought of having to leave her son out in the cold with nowhere to stay, and adding, would someone please see to it that her little girl, Mary, would be taken care of.

The one person that the family turned to in times of trouble was my mam. She was a stalwart and a very strong and hard-working woman. When she heard the news she almost collapsed, but she pulled herself together with the encouragement of my dad, who was the strong, silent kind of man. He was the sort that people would turn to if they got cut or bruised or just needed quiet assurance. He would put on balm and bandage, then we would feel better. The neighbourhood kids were always running to Mr Hill whenever they hurt themselves.

With the help of my Aunt Lil who lived across the road from us and was my mam's staunchest friend, Mam went into action. They went down to Uncle Bert's house. Now I must say that my family were not all close to Uncle Bert. We never visited them, and they never visited us, and they only lived just around the corner from our house. Until that day I didn't know which house was his. When Mam and Aunt Lil got to Uncle Bert's they were shocked to see the condition the house was in. They looked past this and gathered all the children and brought them home to our house. As you can imagine, they were all in a state of shock, and they all came willingly, even thankfully. Now we lived in a three-bedroomed house. There was Mam, Dad, my brother Frank, and me. With this influx of people we were stretched beyond the limit.

The first order of the day was to get everyone a hot bath and clean clothes. It always seemed that with my mam the first thing was a good hot bath. This was really was a healing process, and to my mam very necessary. Mam begged, borrowed and almost stole for these her nieces and nephews. The little girl was the neediest of them all. She was just 3 years old. She was dirty and unkempt. When my mother had finished with her she looked like a little princess. She was all pink and glowing. The comment from the older kids was, "Aunt Mildred, we didn't know what it was like to sleep between clean sheets until we went to bed last night in your house." Once the kids were all settled Mam turned her attention to Uncle Bert. He didn't know what was about to hit him. I'm sure the poor man was in shock. He was saying over and over again, "Why should this happen to me?" and holding his head.

That got my mam's dander up. He had, after all, mistreated the poor Lilly and shown no compassion for her young son. Well, upon hearing that, my mam saw red, and she gave him the tongue lashing of a lifetime. "Why should this happen to you?"

He didn't know what hit him. He couldn't get away fast enough; he left Mam and Aunt Lil there in the house. That was his first big mistake.

Mam and Aunt Lil went through his entire house and were shocked to see the condition the family had been living in. For chairs they had old car seats. The place was filthy dirty. The beds were a shocking mess. No sheets, only dirty blankets. Well, these two tornadoes, Aunt Lil and my mam, moved into action. They dragged all the furniture, such as it was, out of the house, piled it all into a heap in the middle of the back yard. They then found some petrol in the shed where Uncle Bert kept his "darling" motorbike. My mam said he treated that bike better than the people in his household. Well, they poured the petrol onto the heap, and with glee put a match to it. Aunt Lil said that my mam almost singed her eyebrows. It was a whopping great bonfire. It was as good as any Guy Fawkes night bonfire. In this day and age the police would have been there to issue a fine for some violation or other. The flames were raging higher than the house tops, and the smoke could be seen streets away. When Uncle Bert came back to see all his junk burning away in the back yard he was not a happy man. He didn't say too much, as my mam told him, "You can afford to get new stuff, our Bert." I guess he thought that silence was the better part of valour; and I think he was right. He could see she meant business.

Mam and Aunt Lil were tuckered out by now. They had no thought for this one-legged man and where he would stay that night.

They returned home to feed the starving. My mam was quite invigorated, even though smelling of smoke and in need of a good hot bath herself. Mam got in touch with Lilly's family and made arrangements to have the little girl, Mary, adopted by an aunt and uncle who lived in another part of the country. She heard years later that she had grown up to be a lovely young lady. We never saw her again.

Once the funeral was over my mam and her sidekick, Aunt Lil, went on a furniture hunt. They were very determined to get some decent beds and chairs, knowing that Uncle Bert never would. If car seats had been okay before they would not be okay now. Mam was not going to let that happen if she could help it, and she could help it. I think she felt a bit guilty for not keeping in touch with them over the years. The children could move back home and be sure to have a halfway presentable home. The stuff they found they had delivered, and Uncle Bert just had to pay for it. I really think that once he saw the results of their work he was secretly glad that they had taken the bull by the horns. His house was clean for the first time since they had moved in. He did thank my mam and Aunt Lil, and I believe he was truly grateful. All the children did move back with him. All, that is, except Alfred, who rented a room in town, and Margaret, the eldest daughter. She asked my mam if she could stay and live with us. She said she could not go back to that style of living. She stayed at our house until she got married couple of years later to a man named John, who came from quite a wealthy Scunthorpe family.

In the meantime my mam had bought herself a brand new electric washing machine, one of the first in the neighbourhood, so that she did not have to wash clothes by hand anymore. No more dolly tub and dolly legs. That was how she had to do the washing before the machine. When Margaret got married my mam wanted to give her a good start in life, so she paid for most of the wedding. Now how do you think she got the money? Well, she sold her brand-new washing machine, her pride and joy. I do admire my mam for the generous soul that she was. Margaret was also grateful and was very fond of her Aunt Mildred.

After that tragic affair the cousins were a lot closer, and we would often get together. We were more like a family now. So it is true that some good can come out of tragic events.

Whenever I return to Scunthorpe for a visit we all have a grand reunion, lots of old family stories and a lot of laughter.

The Baths

The year was 1950; the war was well behind us, and most rationing was over. My hometown of Scunthorpe had an indoor swimming pool, "the baths." In the winter time hardly any one went swimming, so they emptied the water out and built a retractable floor over the pool. Then they held dances there every weekend. During the week they would have dance lessons or different functions. Later we even had some big-name bands and singers.

But when it first opened it was strictly for dances. On Friday nights the dance was for people under the age of twenty. My brother Frank was sixteen going on seventeen, so he and his friends would go dancing every Saturday. He would come home after the dance was over, come upstairs, open the door to my mam and dad's room, put his head around the door, and say, "I'm home," then go off to bed.

Well, this one particular Friday he didn't put his head round the door, instead he just mumbled "Good night."

Mam thought it was odd but didn't think any more about it. My brother was home; she and Dad could now go to sleep. The next morning Frank was off to work before anyone else was up, so Mam didn't see him until the evening when he got home from work.

When she did see his face his lip was all swollen. She jokingly remarked "What, did she bite you last night?"

The story he related to her really shocked her. I must say that my brother was a very good-looking young man, clean cut and respectable and quiet, not like his sister. He never gave any trouble to his parents.

He had gone to the dance as usual with some of his mates. They met other friends there. One of them was a very pretty girl named

Maureen. She and my brother were almost dating. The two of them were dancing when this stocky young man kept bumping into them. Our Frank could see that there could be trouble, so he told his friends that he thought it best if he went home. So he went to get his coat from the cloak room, then left the building. When he got outside this stocky young man and a couple of his mates were waiting for our Frank. They set about him and knocked him out. While he was on the ground he heard the leader say in an Irish accent, "If he moves we will kick him to death." Well, Frank was nobody's fool, so he stayed on the ground as still as he could. He was not a fighter and was certainly no match for the three of them. When the three thugs saw that there was no more sport they left, and Frank's mates helped him home.

Well, if you knew our mam you would know she would move hell and high water to protect her children. She had her dander up. She spent the week trying to find out who these men were. She questioned all Frank's mates and found out that one of the men was a Scunthorpe lad. And as it just happened it was the son of an old school friend of hers. She went around to see the dad. He was as shocked as my mam, saying that he would sort out his son and get to the bottom of this.

Well, all her efforts paid off. She found out that the assailant was, in fact, an Irish man of twenty-four years of age. At that age he should not have even been at the dance. She told my dad that we had to do things the right way. Off she went to the police station with me in tow. She spoke to the policeman in charge and reported what had happened, asking him to arrest the culprit. The officer said, yes, he could do that, but that might make matters worse, as they could only give him a warning and then he would be free to do even worse.

Mam said, "Well, what if I got hold of him and taught him a lesson?"

There I was at my mother's side saying "Are you going to hit him up, Mam? Are you going to hit him?"

The police man said, "You could do that, but then you could be arrested." While he was saying that he was giving the nod and a wink, as much as to say that they would turn a blind eye. He said that often the public could do more than the police because their hands were tied. One final warning was that these men could beat up my mother.

My mother was determined to set this fellow straight. The following Saturday night she and my Aunt Lil went to the baths armed with two wooden candle sticks stuffed into a big bag. I chuckle when I think of it; it didn't seem very threatening to me. When they got to the baths they were greeted with a lot of funny looks. What were these two old ladies doing at a youth dance? They were all of forty years old. They went to sit on the balcony, having a good view of the dance floor. Frank's mates came over to talk to Mam and Aunt Lil. While they were there the three amigos sauntered in and went to sit at a table on the edge of the dance floor. "Those are the men," they said, and within an instant they were gone. Mam said they were scared to be seen with her, knowing how angry she was.

The dance was going in full swing with lots of couples on the dance floor. These two ladies went over to the Irish man and Mam asked him if he was the one who beat up a young man last week. With a sneer and a shrug he said, "So what if I did?"

"Why did you do it?" my mam asked. "Is it because he is better looking than you and a lot smarter?"

He just shrugged. Mam was getting angry at his attitude, he was so puffed up and full of himself. She called Aunt Lil over, opened the bag, then she grabbed one of the candle sticks and started to hit him over the head. The poor man did not know what happened. He got up and started to run across the floor. The dancing couples were hindering his progress and making way for his assailant.

Mam shouted to Aunt Lil, "Lil, don't let him out of the door!" The door was, in fact, two swinging glass doors so Aunt Lil stuck her hand through the handles. That didn't stop him. He ran straight at the glass and broke through. He was out the door, over the turnstile, and off down the street. The two "ladies" went outside but couldn't see him, so they got on their bikes and went home. They had an exhilarating time. Once they got home and had a cup of tea they realized that they would have some explaining to do to the manager of the baths. They decided to go back and explain things to him.

When they arrived back at the scene the manager was in a right stew. He was concerned, asking, "Who is going to pay for the glass door?"

As he was saying that, who should come strutting back, but the Irish man.

My mam said, "Well, here he is now; he will have to pay for it." She asked the man, "What on earth possessed you to do that to my son?"

He still had the same cocky attitude. As he stroked a hand over his gloved hand in an exaggerated movement he said, "I was three years welter-weight boxing champion of Ireland."

"Well," Mam said. "This is from no champion!" and she hauled back and punched him in the face.

The man covered his face and said, "No more, Missus! No more!"

Poor Mam; she almost broke her hand. She said, "I know a young lad that said that, lying on the ground with three of you ready to kick him to death if he moved."

We heard later that he was bashed about so badly that he had to take two weeks off work. He was probably humiliated as well.

The people he worked for would not give him his job back. He did manage to find other work as a bricklayer. Frank came home from work one day two weeks later and presented our mam with a box of chocolates. This man was now working at the same company as Frank. He sent the chocolates for my mam with his apologies, saying, "She gave me what I have needed for a long time."

I look back now and think that it could have gone terribly wrong and been a completely different outcome. I would not recommend that anyone else do the same thing as my mam. She was very fortunate to be left standing.

Sentimental Journey

My mother was a hard-working woman. She wanted to give my brother and me everything that she never had. On cold winter nights she would warm our pajamas in front of the fire, and then she would relate to us what it was like when she was a child. We were really enthralled by some of the stories. Some were very sad, as they were really poor, often without proper warm clothing. Some of them were really funny. My mam was a great storyteller. One story that she told us was that they were so poor that she and her two brothers all had boys' boots. You could tell by the leather tag on the back to pull them up. My mam would complain and cry that every one would know they were poor, and because of the tag they would know she was wearing boys' boots. They may have been poor, but my mam still had her pride.

My grandma would say, "Oh! Our Vera, push the tag into the boot, and no one will know the difference." It was a case of the first one up in the morning would grab the best pair of boots.

She and her brothers would each take a sack and walk along the railway track after the coal train had passed. They would pick up any coal that happened to fall off the train. She said sometimes the man who fed the engine would accidentally drop some lumps and give them the wink. Everyone in that part of the country was poor, and they would help each other. This was all prior to World War I.

She actually never went to school after she was eleven years old. She would do babysitting and clean houses. She loved to see a clean house.

Then at twelve she was put into service, or as she would say, "into sarvis." As she was brought up in Middlesborough in Yorkshire, that was how they said it. She was sent to a preacher's home in Sheffield. Grandma thought she would be well treated there in a Christian home, with a preacher, at that. You also would think she would have been treated very well. But that was not the case. There was another girl working there, and Mam was told that they would have to share a room. But it really was an attic with two beds and a curtain to separate them. The mattresses were really palliasses A palliass was a mattress filled with straw or horse hair, and they were very uncomfortable. There was a cover made out of old coats cut into squares and sewn together. At least that was warm. Under that an old blanket was covering the bed. As I recall it now it sounded like the dark ages and always put me in mind of one of Charles Dickens' stories.

Well, Mam was used to hardship, even though this was a bit harder than she thought. It was probably because she was away from her mam. But as she was in a preacher's home she thought she would be treated with Christian kindness. But I guess there are Christians and then there are Christians. She was still determined to do her best. Her first morning there she was up before anyone else, so into the kitchen she went and got herself some bread and jam and a pot of hot tea. When the preacher's wife came down she was horrified and told my mam, "Now Vera, you are only to eat when I say and what I give you."

Mam soon learned that she could not do as she pleased. That she had to learn another way. One day the preacher's wife told her that she was going out and would not be home for lunch that the preacher would be eating lunch alone, so to set the table for one.

Well, Mam did what they were used to at home. She put the table cloth on halfway across the table. No point covering the whole table, as there was only one eating. At home they didn't have table cloths; they had other things they could do with their money, so they would cover the table with newspapers. If there was only one person eating they would cover the table halfway with the newspaper then they could eat and read at the same time. When the Lady came back and heard what Vera had done she laced into my mam, giving her a tongue lashing.

To make matters worse, when the Lady of the house had visitors she related this incident to them. My mam was humiliated.

Well, this "sarvis" was not at all to my mam's liking. She only lasted about two weeks. Then she packed her bag, and early one morning when there was no one about she sneaked out of the house and ran to the train station. When she got to the station she could not buy a ticket, as she had no money. She must have looked a pathetic sight, this little girl with all her worldly possessions in a cloth bag. The ticket man had sympathy on her, as he asked her, "What's up, luv? Are you running away from sarvis?" When Mam answered in the affirmative he let her on the train at no cost. When she did get home my grandma was very happy to see her and vowed that "our Vera" would not go into "sarvis" again.

Then the family moved from Middlesborough to Scunthorpe one year later. Scunthorpe is a steel industrial town, so there was lots of work available. They were still dirt poor—so poor, in fact, that my grandma didn't have a wash tub; no washing machines in those days. She would use the metal garbage can to do her washing in. Every wash day she would first have to scrub out the dust bin (garbage can) before she could do the washing. The garbage collector couldn't understand why her bin was so clean. He would say it is the cleanest dust bin in town. Little did he know what grandma had to do every week, and she was too proud to tell any one.

I was born in Scunthorpe. When I was about the same age as my mam was when she went into service, my mam got a longing to see the place where she had grown up. Her brother Uncle Walt had a black Ford car, nice and new and shiny; he said he would drive her there. It was his early home also, and it was his dream to go back and see the old place. I, of course, didn't want to be left out, so I was to go with them.

We took off one Sunday morning, just the three of us. I had never been on such a long journey. The farthest I had been was to Cleethorpes, the seaside town about 30 miles from home. This was further than that, and I kept asking, "Are we there yet?" Eventually we were in Middlesborough. After turning this way and that we soon found the street where Mam and Uncle Walt used to live. It was an area of about three city blocks. It was row, upon row, upon row of dismal, terraced houses. All of them were right up to the pavement. No garden or plot of land to call your own. As you opened the front door you stepped onto the street. It was not a particularly cool day; in fact it was quite warm. But oh, what a miserable street this was! It was grey and grimy from the coal dust of the coal mines all around. And it was depressing. The street was long and lined on both sides with these dreary terraced houses. One style of house repeated all the way down the street, the same on both sides. No variation, just drab, drab, drab. I remember feeling just a little bit scared. So I stayed close to my mam's side.

I believe the street was demolished soon after this. So this was more or less the last chance to visit the people here. Uncle Walt parked the car, and Mam and I got out. There were scruffy, snot-nosed kids playing on the street. When the car stopped they all came running to see the posh car, putting their dirty hands all over the car and pushing their noses against the windows, eyes wide open as if they had never seen a car before. Uncle Walt was worried that his *lovely* car was getting dirty. Cars were not a common sight in those days; only the rich could afford them, so I suppose Uncle Walt must have been rich.

Mam couldn't be contained; off she went scurrying down the street with me at her heels. I was not about to miss anything, and I was not going to be left on this street on my own. These kids looked pretty rough to me.

Mam looked at me and said, "There, that's the house I used to live in." She was excited, and I could not understand why she was so happy to be on this dingy, dreary street. Next thing I knew she was knocking on the door. When the lady opened the door my mam said, "Hello," then she said, "I'm revisiting the area. You know this is the house that I used to live in."

The lady looked startled and said, "Eh, no luv, you must be mistaken. We've been living here in this same house for 30 years." Then she thought for a while and said, "If my memory serves me right I think the people who lived here before were called the Boneses."

Mam said, "Yes, that's right, I was Vera Bones."

The woman was really surprised. "Eh, to think that you would come back after all these years!" Then Mam asked her if Ellen Johnson, her old pal still lived on the street. The lady said that she lived across the street, but she was now Ellen Baker, and gave us the house number. We went across the street to the house. The front door was wide open. I can still see it now. There in the middle of what I supposed was the front room, was a large kitchen table that had obviously been there many years, and looked as if it had been scrubbed until it was almost white. This looked like it was the only room, but then to the rear there was a door which must have led to another room at the back, the kitchen I guessed. Around the table were several men in all stages of undress. Well, that's not quite true, they were dressed, but only half dressed. They had their pants on. One even had a shirt on. The rest were in their undershirts with braces to hold up the pants. A couple had cigarettes in their mouth or in their hand. On the table were an overflowing ash tray and three large brown bottles. Even I knew that they were beer bottles. The men were very noisy, as they were playing cards and slamming their hands on the table.

When we stood at the door they all looked around. The look on their faces told me that we should not be there. One of them asked in a not too friendly voice, "What do you want?"

Mam asked if Ellen Baker who used to be Johnson still lived here. One of the younger men turned his head to the back of the house and shouted, "MAM!"

With that my mam said, "Are you little Billy?"

He scowled at her and said, "Yes."

"Well," my mam said, "I used to change your nappies when you were a baby." Even this big strong man he had to blush at that. The other men gave a snicker. With that Ellen came from the back of the house rubbing her hands on her apron.

By now my mam was playing the game to the hilt. She said, "I used to live down the street."

"Well," Ellen said, "I'm sorry, luv, I don't remember you."

Then Mam said, "Ellen, it's Vera Bones."

Well, Ellen went into action; she invited us in, gave one of the men a cuff about the ear and told them to give us their seats.

Someone ran off and made a pot of tea and gave it to us to drink.

There was a lot of reminiscing and talk of old times. Even Billy warmed up to the occasion and had a laugh at being taken care of by my mam. He could tell she was one of their own who had gone out into the world beyond these streets and done well.

Mam had told us that when she was little the family were very poor and often didn't have enough food to go around, and there was a lady who owned a corner grocery store at the end of the street. Mam would go to her and say, "Mrs Yates, do you have some bread and jam?" Well, Mrs Yates was a kindly lady and would give her some bread and jam to eat. In return my mam would do odd jobs for her. I think Mrs Yates created jobs for her to do. The kindness of that lady stuck with my mam all through the years. She said to Ellen, "I suppose that Mrs Yates is gone by now."

"Eh, no luv, she is still alive, but ah, she has gone blind." With that she turned to Billy and told him, "Go and get her, and don't tell her who is here; let it be a surprise."

After a little while this big, rough man came back with this feeble old lady on his arm and gently led her to a chair in the room. She was stooped over and looked really ancient to me. When she sat down my mam said, "I bet you don't know who I am."

Mrs Yates said, "Eh, I'm sorry, luv; I'm blind, and I can't see you."

My mam said, "Mrs Yates, do you have some bread and jam?"

What happened next was a complete surprise to me and I think every one in the house. Mrs Yates started to cry. With tears running down her wrinkled cheeks she sobbed, "Eh, lass, it's Vera Bones. After all these years she has come back to see us."

They fell into each others arms, both crying and sobbing. It is quite safe to say that there was not a dry eye in the house.

Even the tough men could not hold back the tears. Uncle Walt stepped outside with the excuse he was watching his car. But we all knew that his eyes were misting up also. Just think how it is possible to have a lasting memory; one that spans the years. And yet is so real and charged with so much emotion. There was lots of reminiscing; Mam ribbed Billy about how she babysat for him and what a luvely bairn he was. Eventually it was time to go. We had to get home before it got too dark. They all said their goodbyes.

I think that every one of them knew it was to be the final farewell.

On the homeward journey we were all very sad that these people had not been able to escape their lifestyle. Ah, well now, that the area was all to be pulled down; they would have to make a change, and it could only be for the better. And my mam was ever grateful that her mother had moved them to our home town. There was no comparison between our lovely little town and that depressed area. I think it is good that it is now gone. Time and progress will win out over all the depression.

I just hope and pray the move made a better life for Ellen Johnson and her family.

Part 2
The Adventures

Australia

The year was 1981. My husband Louis decided that he was going to Australia to meet some of his old school mates who had immigrated there. Now he had left Sri Lanka in 1957 while it was still known as Ceylon. That's the place where the tea comes from. Many of his friends had immigrated to Australia, and he had not seen them since then.

Well, I thought, *if you can go to see your old friends I can go to see my friend Yvonne who had also immigrated to Australia along with her family.* She and I met while working at Butlin's Holliday Camp at Clacton-on-Sea, England. We both worked in the hairdressing salon there.

This was purely a summer job. We later moved to London and shared a flat together. Well, it was really a room, as we could not afford a flat. We even got jobs in the same hairdressing salon, so we really spent a lot of time together.

I got married and moved to Canada, and she married and eventually moved to Australia. We kept up a correspondence for some years. Then time took its toll, and we lost contact.

Now I had not been in touch with Yvonne for quite some time. Her address was just a vague memory. I fished around in my mind until I came up with what I thought was her last address. I wrote to her there, hoping above hope that it would find its way to her. A couple of weeks later I received a letter from her saying, "Thank God, I was praying that you would get in touch." Well, whoever this vague God was, her prayer seemed to work.

Louis made arrangements for us to go just after Christmas. That was January 1982. We were to go to Melbourne. Then he would stay

57

there and visit family and friends while I went to Perth to visit Yvonne. I only had one week to revisit my old friend. I was looking forward to our time together, chatting, catching up on all the news. I was wondering if we would still be the same, or even like each other after such a long time. It had been twenty years, after all, and people do change. I am sure she was just as anxious as I. I landed at Perth Airport and found my friend waiting. It had been such a long time since she last saw me that she didn't recognise me, with my long blond hair. I don't know what colour it was when she last saw me. I changed colours at the drop of a hat in those days. She was walking up to women and asking, "Are you Maureen?" We both had a good laugh, and it was just as if we had not been apart for such a long time. She met me with, "Praise the Lord!"

I thought, *Ay, Ay, what's this?* I knew she was a Catholic, so put it down to "their" way of talking. I couldn't remember her talking that way before.

We made it from the airport in a bone shaker of a car that a friend had loaned her. All the way her conversation was laced with, "Praise the Lord!" and "Thank you, Jesus!"

I thought, *Oh, my goodness! What have I got myself into? Well, I said to myself, Maureen, just grin and bear it is only for one week.* Little did I know that by the end of the week I would not be the same. My life would be completely turned upside down.

It was about an hour's drive to her home. She lived in a place called Innaloo. (I know, it sounds like she lives in the toilet.) I found out that it is an aboriginal name, as many towns are in Australia. Her place was so nice; she lived in a two-bedroom flat. It was unlike the flats in London and unlike the apartments in Canada, and I found it very quaint. It was very sparse, but comfortable. She told me that she and her husband David had divorced, and she had a little girl Elizabeth, who was about three years old, a sweet little blue-eyed blond.

We were chatting up a storm when a kindly friend who had been fishing brought her a very large fish that Yvonne made into our supper.

She lived just a few blocks from the ocean, so the fish was, I think, the freshest I had ever eaten. While we were enjoying the delicious meal the phone rang. It was someone from Yvonne's church. I could only hear one side of the conversation, and concluded that this person wanted Yvonne to go a church meeting this very evening. Now this was a Wednesday night, not a Sunday, and I seemed to be the problem, as I heard Yvonne say "Oh, I would love to come, but my friend is here from Canada. If she will come then I will, but if not then I will stay here with her." Now by this time it had started raining and didn't look like it would ever stop.

I said, "No problem. You go; I will just stay here." I didn't feel like being on my own, but I didn't feel like going to any church either. She wouldn't hear of it. So, after she very craftily made me feel guilty, I ended up going with her. In my mind I thought I was being such a nice person. The truth was more likely to be that all her friends were praying. Anyway I told myself that I would go and keep my eye on what she was up to and what they were doing. She had been telling me her story, how she had been in a very unhappy and desperate state. One evening while praying, she started babbling in some unknown, weird gibberish. She told a friend what had happened and that she thought she was losing her mind. The friend said that she should go to see a lady psychiatrist that she knew. The psychiatrist told her that she had what they called a Pentecostal experience and advised Yvonne to go to a Pentecostal church, as they could explain it better.

I had no idea what that was, but I was sure it was witchcraft or something just as spooky and devious. I mean, like I knew anything about witchcraft. That was enough for me to get my antenna up. Anyway, it was still raining, and didn't look like it was going to cease any time soon. In actual fact it rained and rained all the time I was there, except for one day at the end of the week when we were able to go to the beach.

I was just like a sitting duck to all these Christians. The end result was that I went to church with her. When we got there I was introduced to her newfound friends. They all wanted to hug me, getting in my space. It made me very uncomfortable. There was a coffee shop of sorts, where they gave bread to the poor. I'm sure they gave other stuff, but all I remember was the bread. The place looked as if it had been outfitted by the poor. Rather tatty looking. Not *my* kind of place at all. The more of her church people I met the more hugs they all wanted to give me, getting in my face. I was not at all comfortable with all this huggy, huggy stuff. I was even glad to go into the church to get away from them. We went into the meeting hall. This was not like any church I had ever been in. Not that I had been in many churches. I had been to weddings and one funeral; that's all. Well, this church had been a warehouse, and had three walls and a roof. That caused my guard to go up a notch. I found out later that the man that had owned the property 50 years earlier had been like a hermit and had prayed that his home would become a church. Well, now it was.

The service was about to start. I was not about to join them, so I made up my mind to sit at the very back of the room. Yvonne, of course, sat with me and another lady sat next to her. I supposed this was the lady that had phoned her. There was this great gaping chasm between us and the rest of the congregation, who were in the first two or three rows. Now I look back and laugh at how obvious I was and *very* anti whatever they were. The service started with everyone except me singing. For a start, I did not know the songs they were singing, and I was really surprised, even dumbfounded as they were jumping up and down and waving their arms and hands about. This was really bizarre. Now, I thought that this was really very fishy. Not what a church service should be like. They are supposed to be reverent and dour. I mean, really, how was I to know? I didn't know when I was last in a church. But whenever that was it was a good Church of England church, and they knew how to be reverent.

As the singing continued someone on this back row started to speak in some strange language. Now I knew it was not me, so I looked to see if it was the lady standing next to Yvonne. Oh, no! It was

Yvonne! I could have disappeared into the wall I was so embarrassed. I could not understand what on earth she was babbling about. When she finished a man at the front began to speak in English. The gap between us was too great for me to hear everything he was saying, but I did hear him say something about grasshoppers. This was just too much. It was the weirdest thing to me. What on earth had grasshoppers to do with church? I have since found out that they are mentioned in the Bible in Numbers 13:33, but at the time I thought, *What is all this drivel?* I could not wait to get out of there, and to top it of I was getting a doosy of a head ache. Now I was sure she was into some witchy stuff, and my head ached so much I could not think what to do or say. And I did have lots to say. I was sure my headache was due to the witchy stuff. Can you imagine, I thought that they could have been doing curses or voodoo? Casting spells. It sounds silly now, but then I had no guidelines to follow, and I was very concerned for my friend's well being.

I went outside to get some fresh air, and thought, *When Yvonne comes to look for me she will take pity and we can go home.* Not So. When she came to look for me and found out that I had this awful headache she insisted that Don, whoever Don was, would pray for me. She would not take no for an answer, and she dragged me back inside. I mean, literally, she took my arm and pulled me inside. I never knew how forceful Yvonne could be. So, in order to get out of there as soon as possible and not cause a scene I allowed myself to be ushered inside the church, almost kicking and screaming, which is what I was doing on the inside. I was out of control. I didn't like the feeling.

Don, it turned out, was the pastor. He was a tall, friendly man; I suppose if he had not been friendly that would have been the end of my story. He said of course he would pray for me. Now if they really were into witchcraft that was the worst thing I could allow them to do. What did I know? I was sure I was able to take care of myself. I was such a cocky thing. I stood there in the middle of this church with everyone watching. I'm sure they were not, but it sure felt like were. He put his hand on my head and started to pray. Now I thought I should close my eyes, as that is what you are supposed to do when you are in church, and being prayed for. Once again, how did I know? I had never had anyone pray for me before. The next thing I remember was that I was standing there in the middle of the room (with everyone watching!) when I realised that I had my head on this man's chest. Now how my head got there I will never know. So I thought to myself, *Now, come on, Maureen, if you slowly lift your head up no one will notice.* Yeah! Well, that is what I did. I s-l-o-w-l-y lifted my head. The next thing I knew I was flat on my back on the floor, and I was howling with laughter, a loud, raucous belly laugh.

I kept saying, "Oh, I'm sorry, I'm sorry," thinking, *This is not right in church. Aren't you supposed to look and act dour and serious? Not lying flat on your back howling with laughter.*

All the while they were saying, "Praise the Lord!" and "Halleluiah!" The more they did this the more I saw the funny side of the whole situation and laughed all the more. I had been so miserable for so long; it was good just to have a good laugh. How I got off the floor I will never know. All I knew was that I was a limp mess.

After the service we were to go to Yvonne's friend, Deirdre's house to spend the night. She was going on vacation with a friend and so was loaning her car to Yvonne for the rest of the week. Up to now I had been with one born-again Christian. Now there were two of them. I didn't stand a chance. Anyway, I was curious and had lots of questions for them. Sitting in Deidre's living room I started the inquisition, peppering them with questions. When I say peppering, it could really have been pellets from a shotgun. I was going to get to the bottom of this stuff. Why was every one jumping and waving their hands about? Who pushed me to the floor? Why wasn't anyone cross at my behaviour while lying on the floor, making a fool of myself? Can you imagine I thought that having a good laugh was making a fool of myself?

All these questions were answered, not all to my liking or satisfaction. Then I asked the *big* one. "What is all this talking in tongues stuff?" They tried to explain it to me, but I was having none of it. So I said, "Well, if you can do it any time, *do it now!*"

Well, that threw them for a loop. They looked at each other and said, "Well...."

Now I only found out years later that they were both brand-new Christians. So I was really putting them on the spot. But good little Christians that they were they started by praising the Lord. They went off into praying in tongues. It was then that Yvonne started talking in tongues.

Well, it just sounded different, and as she talked I just started to howl and cry. I just sobbed and sobbed. I was a blubbering mess. Now anyone that knows me knows that is very unusual for me to cry. I have even had Christians look at me to see if I will cry at some sad story or moving song. No, it just does not happen. It could be the British stiff upper lip; anyway this was something very unusual. By now I felt like a blubbering fool.

Now this meant more questions. What was Yvonne saying? They said they did not know.

"Well!" I was completely flabbergasted and somewhat annoyed at making such a fool of myself. "What the on earth good is that?" I asked.

"Well," said Deidre, "we could pray again and ask God what it was." Okay off they went again, chattering in tongues.

Then once again Yvonne spoke out loud, but in English this time, saying "Behold, I stand at the door and knock, and if you will open the door I will come in and sup with you." This also, I found out later was in the Bible, Revelation 3:20. But at the time it made no sense to me. That did it. Once again I started to cry and sob uncontrollably. I was once again a blubbering mess by this time, red eyes red and runny nose, and my headache was back, and I was feeling quite exhausted, absolutely drained. I had to go to bed. Before I did Deidre gave me a

Bible. It was in everyday English, and she said it would be easy for me to read. Like I couldn't read properly? Oh well, off I went to bed. Anything to get away from these two and their god. I was only there so we could pick up the car in the morning. Then we would be touring around looking at sights and would not have time for all this God talk. I had an amazingly restful night. When I awoke the next morning there was some "wonderful" news. The place where Deirdre was to go for her week's vacation was flooded out. The weather was so bad that all the roads to that area were closed. So that meant we had no car. And it was still raining. I was told later that there had never been rain like that on record, and the weather men had been keeping records since the early 1900s. *Who,* I wondered, *or what was causing all this?* We had no car, and it continued to pour down with rain. Once again I was a sitting duck. I can't remember what we did during the days, but I can sure tell you what the evenings were like. Yvonne would invite friends around for supper or just to visit, and what did they talk about? You guessed it, God and Jesus. I just could not get away from it. Her friends were very nice so long as they did not invade my space. And you know that they wanted to hug hello and hug goodbye. I soon learnt how to hug without really hugging. I thought I was being very smart. I suppose it was like hugging a wooden board.

When everyone went home Yvonne and I would sit for hours talking about her newfound faith. I couldn't understand why we were never tired the next morning. Yvonne said that if God is with us He will give us strength for the day. She would hold my hands over the kitchen table and pray. And I had to admit that when she did I could really feel something different. It was quite electric. I asked her how she learnt to pray like that. She said it was just talking to God, that she had not learnt it; it just happened. I asked if I could do the same. She said yes, all I had to do was talk to Him as if I was talking to a friend.

Well, that very night when I went to bed I had the strangest fear come upon me. It felt like invisible hands pulling and tugging on me. And I sensed faces at the window. It was really quite chilling.

Now let me take you back one year, while I was in Sri Lanka on vacation. My husband and sons had all left that evening to return home to Canada. I was staying with our friends Iris and Thaw. I had been in bed for some time when I was awoken by someone or something hugging me. At first I thought that either Iris or Thaw had come in to hug me good night. This did not make sense, as we had all said our goodnights as we went to bed. We had retired at about 11p.m. I guessed that it was now about midnight. As I became fully awake I realised it was not them at all. Now this was not a normal hug; in fact it was quite violent. I put it down to imagination. I tried to go back to sleep, and again this hugging sensation.

Now this sure was different. I could now feel a presence over my body pressing on me. I had no thought or knowledge of prayer to come against this thing. So I just said, "Get away, get off!" I did the only thing I could think of. I imagined that the whole bed with me on it was covered in a mosquito net. Every night I was there I went through the whole ritual of the mosquito net. This I did in order to sleep at night. The next morning I told Iris what had happened. She thought it had been a dream, but I insisted that it was quite real. When Thaw came home from work that evening I told him what had happened. Thaw said he had heard of this kind of thing before, and said that the locals call it the prince of darkness. He even knew of a woman whose husband was away in India working, and this thing visit her every night.

It seems that this thing only visits women who are separated from their husbands for whatever reason. My husband had left that very evening. Now in the back of my mind I figured out that if this evil was real then there had to be some good because, I reasoned, everything has opposites, hot cold, light dark.

So now here I was one year later with these hands pulling on me. Now I remembered my reasoning one year earlier. This felt evil, so there had to be good. I remembered Yvonne telling me how good God is and that I could talk to God anytime I liked. I had nothing to lose. So I said, "Hey, God, I am afraid. You have got to help me!" I didn't say, "please would you?" I said, "You have got to." Wow!. Yes, now I say, WOW! How irreverent.

To my surprise I heard a voice in my head saying, "Go read the Bible."

I said yes, I would read the Bible tomorrow.

Again, "Read the Bible. Read the Bible."

This went back and forth several times. So in the end I said, "Okay, okay."

Now the Bible that Deidre had given me was in my suitcase at the bottom of the bed. I really had no intention of reading it. I had tried once years earlier to read the Bible and found it boring. So very gingerly I got out of bed. I still had this horrible fear of these invisible hands. I rushed to the other end of the room, opened my suitcase, pulled out the Bible, and jumped back into bed, pulling the covers up to my chin. Now I had the Bible, but what was I to do with it? Earlier I had flicked through it and saw on the first few pages, pictures with headings such as, "If you are unhappy," or "If you are afraid [Ah, that was mine,] turn to Psalm 27."

Well, I was afraid, and I said to myself, *Where the* heck *are Psalms?* I opened the book, and there was Psalms right in front of me. I started to read 27, and when I got to verse 3 I was astonished, to say the least. It read "Though an host should encamp against me My Heart Shall Not Fear."

That was what I needed to hear. From that point on I was not afraid, and I could no longer feel the hands. I said, "Thank you, God." Then I said something that I did not understand; it was not in English. I put my hand over my mouth. *If I start talking like that people will think I am loopy or am having one of these Pentecostal experiences.* So I shut up and went to sleep. I was awoken the next morning with a Christian tune going through my head. "Halleluiah, halleluiah."

No matter how hard I tried not to do it, every morning after that I awoke to some hymn going around in my head. I came out of the room humming.

Elizabeth, Yvonne's little girl, said, "Oh mommy, Maureen is a Christian!"

I still was not convinced, but thought I was just being influenced by them all.

My last night there in Perth before returning to Melbourne, Yvonne invited her friends for a farewell supper. Before they left Michael asked if they could pray for me. By now I was getting used to this prayer stuff, so I said yes. He asked me what I would like the Lord to do for me. Now I had been very unhappy for a long time. I said that I would like to have happiness the way that Yvonne had. I knew that she did not have a lot of worldly things, but she was one of the happiest people that I knew. She always had a smile on her face and a kind word.

He said, "Okay," and prayed for me to have the joy of the lord.

One year later, looking back on this, I realised that I did have the joy of the Lord since that time.

That night after they had all gone home Yvonne and I sat at her kitchen table talking. I told her I did not want to go back to Louis.

She said, "We can pray for him."

I said, "No way. I'm not going to pray for this man who has been so responsible for my unhappiness."

She said, "Very well. I will pray, and you can just sit and listen."

So that's what I did. The one thing I remember her praying was that God would put a song of praise in Louis' heart and that he would sing all day long. I went to bed that night with thanks for what the Lord had done for me in one week, even though I did not fully understand it all. With a heavy heart I wondered what would await me on my return to Melbourne.

The next day I flew out of Perth airport. A few hours later I arrived at Melbourne. Louis was there to meet me. He had been golfing, as usual, and still had his golfing gear on and clubs in the car. After saying our hellos and getting on our way, he said to me, "You know, the funniest thing, I have been singing all day. While going around the golf course. I have been singing "Jerusalem, Jerusalem, lift up your banners high."

Well, I thought, *isn't this amazing; that's just what Yvonne had prayed the night before. This must be the time to tell him of my amazing experience.* I took a deep breath and said, "Louis, I have decided that I am going to be a Christian."

He blew me away with his response when he said, "Good, now maybe you will behave."

That was it. I could have punched him on the nose right there and then, but as he was driving I controlled the urge. We finished our vacation, Him playing golf, and I sitting alone reading the Bible. I read with a newfound fervour, and I really understood what it said. Years earlier I had tried to read it and found it boring. Not any more. Now it was food to my spirit.

Once back in Canada I remembered Deirdre and Yvonne's advice to find a good gospel-preaching church. I didn't know any, so I looked in the telephone directory to see one close to where I lived, then picked up the phone and called the one closest to home. I now have pity on the person who answered the phone, because I bombarded him with the questions that my friends had told me to ask.

Q. Are you a gospel-preaching Church?

A. Yes.

Q. Do you believe Jesus died for our salvation?

A. Yes, we do.

Q. Do you believe in the blood of Jesus?

A. Yes.

Q. Do you believe in speaking in tongues?

A. Yes, we do.

I said, "Thank you very much," and just hung up on him. My mind was made up. This was where I would go. It just happened to be the very place the Lord wanted me to be, Lakeshore Evangelical Church. I grew in that church. The other people ministered not only to me but to my husband also.

When I first started to go to church I had no idea about tithing. On Sunday morning I asked Louis for some money to give the tip. I really was green around the edges. The time came for me to make an open confession of my faith. The pastor gave an altar call; I was the only one to go forward. As I stood there I raised my hands and said, "Holy Spirit, I open the door to my heart; please come in." Next thing I was on the floor. People came rushing to pick me up. Poor things did not know what had happened to me. I said, "Thank you, Lord, for my week of teaching at the hands of baby Christians Yvonne and Deirdre."

Now you would think, *Wonderful, now everything will be plain sailing.* Wrong.

One day the pastor called me into his office. I thought, just a usual visit to see how his new congregant was doing. Again, *wrong.* Instead he asked me how everything was at home.

What a strange question, I thought. It must have shown on my face.

He said that my husband had called the office and accused him of having an affair with me.

Well, I bust out laughing. I think that put him at ease. Even now as I write this I have to laugh. What a silly thing for Louis to think. And for him to accuse the pastor of such a thing was completely out of character. Louis had been brought up as a Catholic and had become completely disillusioned with religion. He hated my going to church. Consequently my Christian walk was without my husband.

This is where I must thank Karen and Gary Damron. They took me into their lives, their home, and their hearts. Being a single woman going to church you are looked on with some suspicion by couples. I and many others like me do not fit into the married group, being minus a believing husband, and having a husband, we do not fit into the singles group. So without the friendship and fellowship the Damron's offered I would have been very lonely, and on the outside looking in, so to speak. Their home was a haven for me to retreat to when I was lonely or when I needed to heal.

Louis went on his own merry way. His love was for golf. When we did bump into each other he would rail at me about all Christians. He did some really bizarre things, things like the phone call to the pastor. We were at home one evening when he started on his rampage about Christians. I was shocked to see him throwing what could only be called a tantrum, stamping his feet and saying, "I hate Christians! I hate Christians!"

I could see that this was not going to stop, so I took authority over whatever that was and told it to shut up in the name of Jesus.

To my utter amazement he stopped dead in the middle of his tirade, sat down and continued to talk about something else as if nothing had happened. His whole countenance changed. That was my first encounter with the enemy, but it was not to be the last.

Louis spent so much time on the golf course that his business partner took advantage and embezzled money out of the company, running it into bankruptcy. This was just more ammunition for Louis to attack Christians, and that of course meant me, even though this partner was not a Christian, in fact he was a Hindu.

This was one of the lowest times in my Christian walk. I was beaten down. I gave in and said, "Okay, I will not be a Christian anymore if that will make you happy." I took the Bible and stood there in our living room and tore every page out. Then I threw them on the floor.

This shocked Louis. I was amazed at his shock. All he could say was that it was heresy for me to do such a thing. I stopped going to church, stopped going to Bible study. I stopped everything. I was not happy; it was as if I was in a fog.

Thank God for true Christian friends. Louise, an Anglican lady friend, called me to have lunch with her. Well, I can always eat. So I met her at this little restaurant. During the meal she said that we should pray.

I said, "No way, prayer doesn't work." I said that God has his favourites, and I was not one of them. I really did think that God had his favourites. I knew of other people who had become Christians, and within months their whole family converted. Louis was still not a Christian, and he was not likely to become one any time soon. I said no.

She took absolutely no notice of me and laid her hand on my shoulder and prayed in the Spirit.

That was all I needed. The peace of the Lord settled upon me. From that point on nothing can turn me from my Lord.

The Trip to Yala

On my husband Louis' retirement we decided to migrate back to his homeland of Sri Lanka. Sri Lanka is a beautiful country, and we looked forward to making our home there. Unfortunately, Louis died of lung cancer after we had been there less than one year. His dream was cut short. His brother and sister, and our sons Mark and Garry came from Canada to be with us through the later part of his illness and were here at the time of his death. After the funeral all but Garry returned home.

Garry had another two weeks before he had to get back to Canada and work. We decided to take a trip to Yala, the national game reserve. Yala is on the southern-most tip of the Island. It is not that far. If we think in Canadian terms it would take maybe three hours to get there, but this trip would take us all day.

We made arrangements to go there for the weekend and set off quite early on the Saturday morning. It is always better to set off earlier and so miss some of the traffic, which can be quite scary. It is amazing how the peace and quiet of early morning can burst into the cacophony of the day. Things to watch out for are, of course, the other vehicles. The drivers are a law unto themselves and will dart in and out, hooting and tooting their horns. It is a constant beep, beep, beep. My son Leroy says the cars in Sri Lanka should have automatic honking systems built in to honk every few seconds whether it is needed or not. They cut you off whenever there is the least space in the traffic. You can be driving down the road in the correct lane when there may be a car or even bus coming straight at you, only swerving at the last minute. Consequently, some of my driving was done with eyes tightly closed. Other hazards can be cows and goats crossing the roads as if they have the right of way. Once in busy Colombo traffic we saw a cow standing between two parked cars, poking its head out and looking this way and that as if to see if the road was clear before crossing the road.

The locals say, "See? Even our animals are smart." Could it be because they think it is a long dead uncle or other relative? Bullock carts also are not unusual, and are even quite numerous.

There are many cyclists zigzagging all over the road with their heavy loads that hide them completely from view. They are so very unpredictable and can turn this way or that without any warning. Even if they did stick their hand out to turn, which they don't, you could not see it behind the heavy load. So I guess their theory is, why even bother? These cyclists can carry loads of almost anything from crates of live chickens to batiks and even clay pots, all tied up with coarse coir rope, destined for the stores. I often wondered how many of them got to the stores in one piece. There is always the condition of the road itself. Now let's not forget that years of neglect have left them in a very sorry state, with many pot holes. We had to be on our toes. Keeping an eye open for all these distractions can be very tiring. All that to stress how important it was to get an early start, and hopefully we could avoid some of the rush.

About half way there we came upon road construction, all very orderly. It was a Canadian project, and looked quite western and efficient, except for the hand painted sign that said:

SLOW MEN
AT WORK
instead of

SLOW
MEN AT WORK

I don't know who painted the sign, but it gave us a good laugh.

The trip went really well. It is a beautiful drive with the road running close to the ocean most of the way. The sun and smell of the sea is so embracing and something I will always remember. We passed by the beautiful seaside resort of Hikkadua, a lovely little town right on the coast. Hikkadua is a haven for hippy-type tourists, very quaint and friendly. We stopped at the hotel to have breakfast. There you can take a glass-bottomed boat ride or snorkel on the reef. The ocean was calling us to go for a swim and see all the beautiful coloured fishes. That was out of the question. We still had a long way to go. In actual fact it is less than 190 miles to Yala, but due to the conditions it takes a full day of driving.

There was an alert situation due to the civil war between the Tamils and Singhalese. If we had known that this part of the Island was a Tamil stronghold we probably would have thought twice before embarking on this trip. When we got halfway there we were stopped at an Army check point. They wanted to check our papers, passport and such. Garry showed his passport while I fished in my handbag for mine. Oh no! I had changed my purse before leaving, and all my papers were in my other purse at home. I had to tell the soldier that I had just buried my husband, Garry's father, and that we were going to Yala for the weekend. The soldier was very severe. He made us pull off the road and get out of the car. He said that we would have to leave the car and take public transport back to Colombo to get the documents. Garry was quietly seething. I think if he could have bonked me on the head he would have done it. Now I really was panicking. If I left the car I would for sure never see it again. The soldier went across the road to their headquarters. The headquarters was just a corrugated tin hut with another soldier standing on guard duty; I couldn't help thinking he must have been cooking in the heat.

While he was gone I said to Garry, "Do you think I should offer him some money?" That, after all, is the way things seem to work here.

Garry was horrified. He said, "No way! We could both end up in jail!"

The soldier came back, still looking very stern. He said, "We will allow you to go on, provided that you promise to report to the police in Colombo the morning you get back. Or else," he said, "they will come and arrest you."

We said thank you and continued on our way. Garry was in a blue funk by now.

Things here are quite different to Canada; at that time you could cross the border into the U.S.A. with only a driver's licence. There was no telling what else was ahead. We wondered if we would run into any other service check posts. We had no permission slip or anything to show we were allowed to continue on our trip. We continued on our way with a certain amount of trepidation.

We were, by now, getting close to a place called Katteragamma. This is where the Hindu pilgrims go to worship the god by that name, quite a horrifying god, by what I had heard. I saw a picture of it one time. It looked like a female with a necklace of sculls around its neck, a headless dead body in one hand, in the other a person obviously still alive with its head being bitten off by this god, and blood all around. You can be sure we made no side trip to see this thing.

The traffic was getting worse. There were a lot of tour buses, and they were driving like mad men. Garry's theory was that they were coming and going to this temple and they must have thought they were under some kind of protection, so could drive like a bat out of hell. That's where they were coming from, and that's just how they were driving, like a bat out of hell. We continued until we got to the fort city of Galle. As we were hungry we made the stop here. Galle is a very clean walled fort that looks out onto the ocean. We went to have lunch in the old colonial-style hotel that has not changed very much since colonial times. The high ceilings, dark wood and big heavy ceiling fans all set the atmosphere. The waiters all dressed in their white sarongs, rushing about, looking really efficient. That is just a facade. What you order is not necessarily what you get. Ask for a coke, you are just as likely to get coffee. After lunch we went for a walk on the ramparts of the fort. The walls of the fort seem to jut right out into the ocean. The warm sun and soft sea breeze takes you to a different time.

Standing there with the soft warm breeze blowing on my face is now burned into my memory. The sea is a lovely aqua blue. You can see the pole fishermen out there on the ocean. I was quite astonished when I first saw them. I had been told about the pole fishermen but thought the report was a bit exaggerated and even unbelievable. Garry's response was the same as mine. There are these scantily dressed men literally out in the ocean sitting atop poles; no real platform, just a bit of wood for them to sit on. What patience and serenity and what balance! I wondered how they even got up there. I could never do it. They can sit there for hours in the baking sun with their fishing poles in their hands. As much as we would like to have stayed and taken in all that the fort had to offer we had to be on our way.

It is amazing how the scenery can change so much in such a small island. In this crowded island I was used to seeing one town run in to another; people bustling all over. Now it was getting more and more like countryside, and more arid and desert like. That meant the roads were worse, but at least the traffic was less. We stopped at a small, nondescript hotel and had a snack. Then we were on our way again.

When we got to the Yala turn off we thought we were at the end of bad roads. Ha! You couldn't call it a road. It was a dirt track with really deep ruts. Garry decided now was a good time for him to take over the wheel. It was another few miles before we spotted the roof of a bungalow that was our motel. It had an open-air dining room, so we got the sea breeze while eating. Just a few yards away from the dining room there was a small lake. Lots of wild animals came to drink, and the monkeys were very cheeky. If you didn't watch they would snatch the food right off your plate. We tourists were really to blame; we just love to feed the animals. It was so relaxing that the guests would gather there to chat and watch the antics. We were shown to our rooms then back to the dining room for a good meal. It was very impressive. The food was good, and the service excellent, I think the best so far.

When we had finished our meal the waiter said to us, "Come, come, come, quickly come." In Sri Lanka it is the habit of the people to repeat things two or three times, such as, "Yes, yes," or "No, no." Anyway this man was very insistent that we follow him to the back of the motel. What we saw there really took our breath away. Standing there with its head in the kitchen door was this giant of an elephant. Now when I say giant, let me try to explain. This elephant's back was as high as the tourist bus parked nearby. The kitchen staff had, over the years, been feeding him tidbits. They fed him all the peelings from bananas or pineapple skins. When they didn't give him enough he put his head in the door again, insisting on more, and they weren't about to say no. The waiter said his name was Half Tail. We could see why; he only had half a tail. He really was a great, lumbering thing. It was a bit scary, as he was, after all, a wild elephant. When he had his fill he turned and lumbered off, his monolith body swaying from side to side, his little half tail swinging at his back.

Years later when back in Canada, I saw a documentary on Yala. The star of the show was, you guessed it, Half Tail. There he was on my TV with his head stuck in the kitchen door and his half tail wagging. It was like seeing an old friend, and it took me back to this time in Yala. I felt that seeing Half Tail would be the highlight of our trip. Boy, was I wrong.

Our rooms were sparse but very comfortable. I fell asleep to the sound of the sea splashing on the nearby beach. The following morning we awoke very early to bright sunshine, as usual. The sun rises at 6 a.m. and we had to be ready for our day's outing that was to start at 7 a.m. We went into the dining room and had a hearty breakfast. The evening before going to bed we had made arrangements for a guide to take us through the wildlife park. As the motel was out of the park limits we got a ride to a little shed where the officials were set up to issue our permit to go into the park. Even though I lived in Sri Lanka, I was still considered a tourist, so had to pay the tourist price, which is very cheap anyway.

There was an open-topped land rover waiting for us, with a driver and our guide. Even though it was very early in the morning it was already getting warm. The thought of sitting in that open truck was not very appealing to me. For Garry's sake I put on a brave face and my faithful floppy red hat. We started off down this bumpy trail. After all, we were in the middle of the jungle, and it sure felt like it.

After the journey of the previous day I could just as easily have sat on the beach and lapped up some sun. We saw some buffalo and a few antelopes. Then on the road, the guide pointed out where an animal, he said probably a leopard, had killed and eaten a porcupine. There were blood and quills and not much else strewn over the road. The guide picked up some of the quills and gave them to me. They were about 12 inches long. I still have them on display in my home. I thought to myself, *Well, isn't this exciting. Ho Hum.* Still couldn't see much of anything. Then in a hushed voice the guide told the driver to stop. He pointed to the bush, and in a whisper told us to be quiet. There, about 40 or 50 feet away, was a group of elephants. It looked like three mothers, three adolescents, and three babies. They were just grazing and eating the tops of the trees and grass as if we were not even there. It was very interesting to see how they pulled up clumps of grass, then knocked the earth off on their feet before eating it. After looking at this for a while I said, "Okay, let's move on."

The guide told me to shush. As we watched they started to move closer. The guide now got out of the truck and was standing at the rear of the vehicle between the elephants and the truck. I thought to myself, *What good could he do? If the elephant wanted to, it could knock him over with one swipe of its trunk.* The elephants came even closer. The big one came right up to within a few feet of us. The driver was getting quite antsy, wanting to leave this place. He knew that the least unusual sound or movement could startle the elephants. He told us later that even the sound of the truck revving up could set them off. Now the guide was making funny guttural noises. The biggest elephant raised its trunk and reached it out towards Garry. The tip of its trunk was only about 2 feet away from Garry's face.

The guide made some other noises, sounding like grunts and growls. The elephant slowly moved backwards, and seemingly very unconcerned, continued to eat the grass. All the elephants then formed into a circle with the babies in the center. That was time for us to leave, very carefully. The guide indicated to the driver that we should move off. The driver was not sorry to go, I can tell you. He told us later that the guide had a knack of talking to the elephants. And as strange as it sounds it did seem like that's what he was doing while he was out of the truck and making all those funny noises. It is considered by some as a sort of gift, a bit like the man who talks to horses. That would have put fear into the driver as something unnatural and to him, even spooky.

We drove around some more and saw other animals; a couple of deer and a leopard way off in the distance, but nothing could top what we had seen. Also in the distance there was another herd of elephants. They were climbing up a small embankment, and one of the babies was having a hard time. One of the large elephants was giving it a push with its trunk. We both thought, *Ah, how cute.*

We went back to the licence shed, thanking the guide, because without him we would not have had this wonderful experience. To say thank you is all very well. We also gave him and the driver a good hefty tip.

Our day was complete, so we headed back to the motel for the afternoon meal. I went back to my room and had a little siesta. Later we went for a walk on the beach. The ocean at this end of the island is much rougher than up in Colombo, so it was very nice just to sit and watch the sunset before dinner, and listen to the sound of the crashing waves. The next morning we were to make our way home.

The trip home was just as beautiful, interesting, and hazardous. We took a more leisurely drive back. We stopped at a batik factory, where Garry bought some for gifts. Then we visited the home of a famous man who made devil masks. Along the way in the little villages were women with spinning wheels making rope out of coconut coir. They were all smiling and happy. Because the return journey was more leisurely we stopped often at the roadside stalls to buy some of the tasty morsels. This certainly is a bountiful Island. We enjoyed taking in the sights of this, my beautiful adopted home. From now on I would be here alone. All my family were back in Canada. It was exciting, and I was looking forward to more trips and adventures.

We arrived home late in the evening with lots of memories buzzing around in our heads. I forgot to report to the police station on our return. I never heard another thing about it. Any how, that's the way things work in Sri Lanka.

Now, after the devastation of the Tsunami, I look back at that time. Will it ever return to that natural beauty I remember so vividly? I see the images on TV and it breaks my heart. Oh, my beautiful Island!

Trip to the East Coast

I had been living in Sri Lanka for some time and was looking forward to seeing some of this beautiful country.

My friend Iris, her husband Thaw, and I made arrangements to go to the east coast. Thaw was the head of security for the Bank of Ceylon. He had to go to Trincomali on bank business. Iris and I were able to go along for the ride.

Iris, Thaw, and I left Colombo early in the morning. It was still dark out. Now apparently the tradition is that when you are going on a long road trip you have to stop at the little roadside caddies, or as we say cafés, and buy Hot rottie and bananas. When I say "hot," that does not only mean warm from the oven but also chilli hot. So who were we to break with tradition? We stopped and stocked up on rotties, bananas, and Elephant House soft drink. Now we were set to go out of town.

The distance from Colombo to Tricomali is about 80 miles as the crow flies, Colombo being on the west coast and Trinco on the east. We had to cross the mountains. The locals call it Up country. They would say they are going Up country to...say...Kandy, or Hatton, and as we had to pass that way I said we were going Up country. In the west this trip would take a couple of hours. In Sri Lanka it is a day trip. Part of the reason is that we made so many stops.

The traffic in Colombo can be very hazardous with the bullock carts, and cars being driven by what seemed like mad men swerving in and out of traffic, with a constant toot, toot, tooting of their horns. It seemed like a constant noise. Men on bikes taking their goods to market loaded down made you think they would topple over. Even early in the morning it is bustling.

OUR MAUREEN

Once we got out of the city proper we could relax a little. There is a famous sweet shop selling all the local candies, all with strange names, such as Talugalla, a little sausage-shaped sweet in wax paper. It is an acquired taste, and I had acquired the taste. Of course we had to buy some. Then a little while later we had to buy some fresh pineapple, all cut and peeled. If you have never tasted fresh pineapple, you have not lived.

The scenery on the way is very different from what we see in the west. There were patches of green paddy fields with little raised paths leading from the village to the farm houses. Around the paddy field are coconut estates. One of the strangest things I have ever seen is the men tapping the coconut to get the toddy. Toddy is the liquid they collect. It is left to ferment. It then becomes quite a potent drink. Now the way they collect it is something else. The toddy tapers tie two ropes from one tree to another way up near the top of the trees. Then they climb up one tree to tap the coconut. How do they do it? I don't know. Then they walk from one tree top to the other by means of ropes, carrying their little pots of toddy. They are like tight-rope walkers without the safety net. They can be 40, 50, or 60 feet in the air. I would rather they than I. It is really something to watch, particularly how they climb up and down the trunk of the tree. I have since seen how they do it. They tie a rope in a loop, then put both feet in it and use that to give them leverage. Pushing with their feet they go up the tree in little jumping movements. They get to the top in no time at all. Now I have tasted toddy fresh from the tree. It is a strange drink. It kind of tastes like drinking a soft drink, while at the same time the aftertaste is like a drink of rubber. The problem was that it started to ferment in my stomach, which was not very pleasant. I felt like I was going to explode. I would not like to taste it again; once is enough.

All over the country side are Buddhist temples with yellow-robed monks walking about. These village temples are usually the size of a house, with a parapet wall around them. They are decorated often with yellow cloth and other bright colours looped and tied all over the place. I believe they represent the prayers of the faithful. It is very fascinating to see the monks going about with their begging bowls. They still do that. They go from house to house, and people are to give them whatever food they have. So at the end of their trek they can have some nice curry and rice along with cake and fruit, all in the same bowl. Some people even drop coins in to the pot. They are not to complain and are expected to eat all the food, even if it is all mushed up together. It is supposed to keep them humble. Once again I will say, rather them than me.

Thank goodness we were blessed with a driver and a company car, as the roads are pretty treacherous. The scenery was absolutely beautiful, and it was nice to be able to see it all instead of having to drive and concentrate on the road. We made pretty good time until we got to a place called Kurunegala. The English used to call it Curnigalle. Someone said that they thought that was how it was pronounced. Trust the English to get it all mixed up. Well, in Singhalese, Kurunegala means rock, and upon seeing the place I could understand why. There were huge rocks all over, showing how we were now getting closer to Up country. We decided to stop here for lunch before the trek up.

It was now high noon and getting pretty hot. We stopped at a bungalow, or as they say, rest house. I found out that all the eating places on the road were called rest houses. Once in Colombo I had seen a sign that said "Hotel." I asked my husband where the rooms were. He laughed. It was only a shop, no rooms at all. They had seen a western sign and used that, not knowing what it really meant.

We ordered our rice and curry lunch, being sure to ask for mine to be mild. What a joke. It was pretty darn hot to me. We replenished our soft drink supply and found our driver. They never eat with us. It's a throwback from the colonial days, I think. I also think the drivers like a break from their passengers. They do these drives many times and make friends along the way. This break is a chance to revisit them, sharing all the local gossip.

We were on our way again and still barely half way to Trinco, so we had to stop a couple of times more. One was to get a cup of tea and give the driver a rest. We stopped way out in the country. No town anywhere in sight, and yet here was this little tea shop. It was quite something. This one was rather dilapidated and not looking very clean. It backed onto a paddy field. The scenery was very green and lush. We found a plain wooden table by a window that overlooked an alleyway.

I said to myself, *Just grin and bear it, Maureen.* I was quite surprised when the waiter brought the cup and saucer, and at the table poured boiling water into the cup, then picked it up and tossed the water out the window. That, apparently, is how they show you it is sterilized. I just hope there was no one walking by the window. They would have got sterilized also. It was a good cup of tea. though.

The trip up the mountains is quite hair raising. The road is only two lanes, one coming and one going. There was not much of a barrier, and the drop was very steep. Most of the road was hairpin bends, and the drivers don't seem to want to slow down. As in Colombo, they drive like their lives depend upon it. All along the way there were little villages, literally the houses and shops were built right up to the road. Sometimes there was only a step to the front door to separate them. Can you imagine having your house, shop, whatever right on the main road with cars and trucks zooming by?

Almost every one we saw had smiling faces. Even with all the hardships they face, they can still smile. It is a lesson for us westerners who have so much of everything, and these people have so little. Because we were getting higher up we had a little rain, quite heavy at times. It was funny to see the people walking with a big banana leaf as a makeshift umbrella: cheap, yet inventive.

We were now getting close to Kandy. Kandy at one time was the capitol of Sri Lanka. There is a lake in the center, and close by it, the Large Buddhist Temple. That is where they keep what is supposed to be Buddha's tooth. I wonder how they got it out of his head? Well, Thaw wanted us to stop here, as he said there was a little restaurant that served the best seafood. Well, talk about seafood, and I am all ears.

We went inside, and Thaw ordered for us. The meal came fast. I think a lot of local businessmen ate here, so they had to be quick. Thaw asked how I liked the cuttle fish. I said it was very good. I had never eaten it before. I have since learnt that cuttle fish is really squid. If I had known that I would have chosen something else. Off we started again as we still had a long way to go before we were at Trincomali.

Iris and Thaw had made arrangements for us to visit some friends of theirs. Thaw had been an Air Force man, and these folks were still in the service. We were now very close to Trinco. I could smell the difference. I knew we were getting close to the ocean. By now I was getting very excited. Iris and Thaw's friends made me feel very welcome.

They had asked Thaw earlier what kind of food I had not tasted since I had been in Sri Lanka. The man had been out hunting especially to get me some wild boar. It is like pork only much, much more tasty. So now I can add that to the list of exotic things I have eaten. We stayed there the night, getting an early start the next morning. I was looking forward to what the day had in store for us. I was excited but not realising what excitement really was. I would find out in a day or so.

Our journey was still not over. We were now in Trincomali. That was, after all, the reason for Thaw being there. He went into the bank while iris and I went for a walk on the beach, which was just across the road from the bank. Imagine working in a stuffy old bank and looking out the window at the sea and sand. The beach was white and wide and went on forever. The only other person on the beach was a young mother and her child playing in the sand. The water was calmer here than in Colombo, and it was calling my name. I had to tell myself, *No, not yet!*

Thaw finished his business for the day, so off we set for Nilavali. Nilavali is about 12 miles up the coast from Trinco. I could hardly contain myself. I had been there previously and knew what to expect. Thaw could not let us go directly to Nilavali. Oh, no. He wanted to show me some sights. I was glad that he did, because shortly after that the war between the Tamils and the Singhalese erupted, and that area was off limits and under curfew.

Thaw is a kind sentimental soul. He wanted me to see where he and Iris lived when he was in the Air Force. I now know why he wanted me to see it. It was a neat little bungalow right on an inlet from the sea.

Iris told me how the elephants used to cross her garden at certain times of the year. One time they stalked through her garden eating all her vegetables. One of them got close to the house and stuck its trunk through the window. The elephants have used the same routes for years. Someone built the bungalow right in their path. Too bad; nothing will stop their migration.

Iris told me that one time, the elephants were on their way to one of the Islands and had to walk into the water to get there. When the water got deeper, they would hold their trunks up in order to breathe. What a sight that must have been.

This was on Air Force land. The Air Force had made a rudimentary swimming hole there with diving platforms. I could not wait any longer. In I went for a quick swim. I splashed about for some time. Iris and Thaw did not want to swim, and I'm sure they thought I was crazy. Then I was told we had to leave. I was none too pleased, but this was Thaw's call. After all, he was kind enough to allow me to come on this trip. So I dried myself off, and we were on our way again.

Next, they then took me to the hot springs. Now that is rather a generous title. It was several cement holes in the ground. They were fed by water from the springs. In each one the water was progressively hotter than the last. As I was salty from my swim, I thought I would test the water so to speak. So with Iris encouraging me, I went to change.

When the locals go in the springs they go in their sarongs or saris. I was shown to someone's office to change, as there was no proper changing room; there was also no proper office either. I had to hide myself behind a filling cabinet to change—away from prying eyes. And there were some prying eyes. Still, I had come this far. I got back into my still-wet swimsuit and ventured out. Well, it was like feeding time at the zoo. There had seemed to be hardly any one there when I went to change. Now they were coming out of the woodwork, or rocks. Anyway, I was the star attraction. All were gawking at this silly white woman in her floppy red hat, and they were grinning from ear to ear. I suppose I did look a bit of a sight. Iris and Thaw were egging me on. They didn't know what a twit I felt. Anyway, I jumped from one hole to another with the appropriate ooohs and aaahs. I couldn't get out of there fast enough. I was still thinking of my lovely Nilavali.

Nilavali

Nilavali was getting closer, but we could not go. Oh no, not yet. Thaw and Iris still had one more sight for me to see. They said it was because we would not be returning this way. This was our only chance to see this sight. We went through a small village up a winding road. Up and up we went to the top of a small mountain. Built high, overlooking the ocean was a Hindu temple. We went inside, mostly to satisfy my curiosity.

These places are rather depressing to me. They are always dark inside. The air is always heavy with the smell of incense and pungent flowers. The people inside seem to think that you there for some spiritual experience. That surely was not the case. With me it was more of an education, a sight-seeing tour. I was curious to see how differently these people worship their gods.

It really does seem to me that they are in bondage after seeing their many gods in that temple, some of them quite fearsome looking, and others daubed with different coloured dyes. They were draped in colourful cloths with very pungent flowers around their necks. The gods could be anything from men to horses or even rats. The way they worshipped was to burn incense, say a few silent prayers, and lay some food stuffs there at the idol's feet. The air inside was really getting hot and heavy with all the different smells. It was time to go outside and breathe the fresh sea air.

I was quite amazed at what I saw next. One of the wooden carved gods, it looked like a little calf, was tossed out on the garbage heap. It had a broken leg, so I suppose it was no longer to be worshiped. It was done for, finished, no longer any good. Still, there is always another to take its place. There are literally thousands of gods that they worship, and I think a lot of them are worshiped out of fear.

Out there on the edge of the precipice was an old gnarled tree almost devoid of leaves, with its spindly branches hanging over the edge. We were at least 100 feet above the sea. We could hear the waves as they lashed on the rocks below. Devotees had gone to the trouble to tie coloured ribbons to the trunk of the tree. Some ribbons were tied to the very tips of the branches. It was so precarious. Just a slight slip could have led to disaster on the rocks below. These ribbons, I understand, are there to represent the prayers of the people. I took pictures of all this, and then I took photos of the discarded god; I got some rather sinister looks. So now was a good time to depart.

Now at last, at last, we were on our way to Nilavili. We had to back track to Trinco then take the road north to Nilavili. It is quite arid out there; not a lot of vegetation except a few shrubs and Arrack palm trees. These are very different from the coconut palms on the rest of the Island. The scenery is quite different from the lush vegetation of the west coast. It didn't take us long to get to our motel off the main road and down a little dirt track.

I had made the arrangements while in Colombo. The owner was a friend of a friend, so we got an excellent rate. We were shown to our room. Iris and I would be staying three nights. Thaw was going back to the Air Force base in Trinco where he would get reacquainted with his old Air Force buddies. We three had supper together; once again the driver disappeared to have his supper.

The dining room was open to the elements on three sides, so as we were eating we could feel the sea breeze and hear the washing of the waves onto the beach. Our meal was fresh shrimp from the ocean. Now you can't go wrong with that. Did I say how much I love seafood? We went for a walk on the beach. It was just so peaceful. There were another couple of hotels a little way down the coast. They were the really fancy, posh tourist hotels. As for Iris and me, nothing could have been better than our little place. Thaw found the driver, then they left for three nights. Iris and I were left to do whatever we liked. I knew that this night I would sleep the peaceful sleep of anticipation

The next morning we awoke early and went for a quick walk to the beach to see the sun rise. We could see out on the horizon where we were to go on this very day, Pidgin Island. This was what I had been waiting for. We made our way back to the dining room and had a meal of rotti, sini sambal and bananas, then arranged with the cook to make us a packed lunch; we took a jug of water, some cookies, and lots of sun lotion for me.

One of the local fishermen had agreed to take us to Pidgin Island this morning. As we carried our stuff down to the water, he was waiting with his little motor boat. There are absolutely no amenities once we get to the island, not even any water. The fisherman would take us, leave us, and then return three hours later. We double checked everything: water, food, lotion, snorkels, bathing suits, and camera. And my faithful floppy red hat. I couldn't go anywhere without my sun hat. We were now ready to go.

The island is about two miles out on the ocean. It is an idyllic spot. It is more or less the shape of a figure 8. One little bay faces south and is more like the ocean, the water quite a bit rougher. The other bay on the north side is very calm water that is full of coral and lots of colourful fishes. The boatman left us on the south side of the island, unloaded all our stuff, and said he would be back in three hours. He looked at us as if we were a bit crazy. He did seem a bit concerned about leaving us all alone. No need to worry. This was our private paradise. Only Iris and me, not another living soul.

OUR MAUREEN

Iris was being very brave, as she could not swim. I think she was prepared to sit on the beach under a tree and wait for the crazy English woman to do her thing. Oh! But once she saw the fun I was having in the water, shouting, "Oh! Iris you should see this one," or, "Oh my, look at that!" she could not resist any longer and came in the water quite bravely. From that point on we were like water babies. The coloured fish, the coral, all the different sea shells, how to explain it in all its beauty? God certainly created some wonderful stuff. I had to smile at Iris, as she got used to the snorkels; she just didn't want to come out of the water. There were fish of every colour imaginable. There was one little fish poking its head out of a hole in the coral, and what looked like a fishing pole growing on the top of its head. On the end of that was what looked like a worm wriggling about. I found out later that's how he catches his supper. Other fishes think it's a tasty morsel, and snap, they are gone. I also saw a moray eel; he kept poking his head out of the rocks. This one was white, not grey like I expected. I suppose this one could have been an albino. Anyway, I felt quite safe. I think he was just as curious about me as I was about him. There was another fish that looked like an upside-down bowl with a frill around the edge, the frill undulating as it moved in the water. I found out later that it was probably a cuttlefish. That's what I had eaten in Kandy that tasted so good.

We were getting hungry, as you can imagine, after all the time in the water. So we sat under a tree and had our sandwiches and drinks. The food was very warm, but what the heck? When you are hungry anything goes. We decided to walk off our lunch. After lathering on lots of lotion we started our walk around the island. That didn't take very long. The width at the widest point was probably about 200 feet, the whole Length about 1,000 feet. The narrowest point was about 50 or 60 feet wide. So we could have surveyed the island in 15 minutes or so. But there was so much to see. The two opposing ends were very rocky, kind of like mini mountains, and as we only had flip flops on we could not climb them. The eastern end of our little plot of land had no beaches and no way around. The western end, on the other hand, was very pretty, and for the size of the island had quite a large beach made up entirely of broken-off coral as white as white could be. Thank goodness for the flip flops. This end was completely exposed to the midday sun beating down on us. So we were in and out of the water trying to cool off.

That was not an easy project, as the ocean was warm, even more warm than tepid. We headed back to our picnic spot, picking up some pretty shells on the way. We also saw something really unusual. There on the beach was this fish, all blown up like a football, with spikes all over it. It had been washed up and was dead, so we poked it about a bit. Iris said she thought it was a blow fish. Well, I couldn't argue with that. It certainly looked like it was blown up. We went back to our little bay and our leisurely snorkeling. We heard the motor of our lift back and knew our time was up. I was almost disappointed having to return to Nilavili. Really, though, that was enough sun and sea for one day. The fisherman told us that he could take us down the river the next day to see the crocodiles. So we agreed to go the next morning. For the rest of this day we just hung out. After a shower and change of clothes we felt more refreshed. We went for a walk along the beach, stopping at the posh hotel for a cool drink. We were served on the patio under the palms. Oh! This was truly a paradise.

We had supper in our own motel, where we were treated more like family. Once more the food was fresh and tasty. We sat there and talked to the other people for a while. The locals are really interesting to talk to. Then, getting more tired, we went to our room, changed into our pyjamas, put on all the beauty creams, then sprayed the room and the patio with mosquito repellent. This has to be a nightly ritual. Can't let them critters get the upper hand. Then Iris and I sat outside chewing the cud until we could no longer keep our eyes open. We went off to bed and another sleep of the blessed. Yes, we really were blessed.

Crocodiles

The next morning was a little more leisurely, getting a later start than the day before. We were quite excited, though; today we would see the crocodiles.

The fisherman arrived on schedule. I must explain the boat was not a very big one. It was really a rowboat with a motor on the back. As I look at it now a big croc could have taken a bite out of it, no problem. Ignorance is bliss. So we had to trust in God to take care of us. We would only be gone a couple of hours. Still, we would be like sitting ducks under the hot baking sun. So once again it was time to check all our needs. Top priority was water, then sun lotion, and my trusty red hat. Iris even brought a sun umbrella, parasol, they say. *How silly,* I thought, but then realised she must have thought me one strange sight in my floppy red hat.

We got into the boat ready for our adventure. We had to take the coast for about three miles. We passed a little fishing village. The people are migrant fisher folk. They would fish on this side of the Island of Sri Lanka at certain seasons. Then they would up and leave, going to the west side of the island. How they got there I was never told. They went up the river possibly. They would stay there for the season then move back again. Their needs were very few, and their homes very rudimentary, what we would call shacks. They left them behind, and when they returned they did whatever repairs were needed and moved back in. With all this they were a very happy people. Their lifestyle was much to be desired. If only they had a comfortable bed and chair, and of course running water, maybe a fan or two. Oh, I could go on. Then they would have all the worries we western folk have. We could see their fishing nets laid out on the beach and one or two men doing whatever repairs were needed. Very often they go fishing at night, returning home the next morning, selling their catch at the hotels close by. The fact that our fisherman was taking us on an excursion was a little more cash for their needs.

The fishing boats were very different from this motor boat. Made from hollowed-out tree trunks, they were long and narrow. They were maybe a foot and a half at the widest part. They had a couple of bamboos poles fastened across the middle and out over the side of the boat. On the ends of that a log was fastened. This acted as a float and stabilizer, so the boats were really quite steady in the water. This was the place that our fisherman was from. He was a strong, hardy man. Now I could understand why.

Eventually we came upon the river estuary. That was where we were headed.

It was very pretty scenery, not at all inhabited. The further we went the scenery changed. It is really amazing how fast the landscape can change in such a small island. It did not seem to be inhabited, as all we saw were a couple of fishing boats tied on the side of the river. With all the greenery about it was fairly cool and pleasant. It was a very peaceful ride. We did not see hide nor hair of even one crocodile. We did, however, see a couple of tracks on the river bank where the crocodile had slid in and out of the water. We also saw the reeds moving about a bit. Our driver said that was a crocodile, and it did sound as if it could have been. We decided to return to our motel. Our quest had not been very successful, but in this land there is always something unusual to see. This day was no different. On our way back down the river we saw the most amazing thing I have ever seen in my whole life. There, crossing the river in front of us, were about 8 or 10 women, each carrying a large bundle of sticks for fire wood on their heads. So you say what is so unusual about that? Well, there was no bridge across the river. These women were walking chest deep in the river. Now remember, this river is known to have crocodiles living there. When they saw us they started shouting and laughing. They must really like their work…. Neither of us knew what they were saying, as they spoke Tamil. I have heard since that when you go into a river where there are known to be crocodiles you must do it very slowly and quietly. These were doing neither, throwing caution to the wind by shouting to us. I was relieved when I saw that they all got out of the river on the opposite bank. The fisherman said that they do this daily. I wondered, *Don't they have wood on their side of the river?* I also wondered how many of them had become crocodile fodder? That really seemed like living life on the edge. We returned to our motel with no further incidents.

The rest of the day was spent very leisurely, swimming, eating, and lazing about on the beach. After supper and all that sun we retired to our room early just to spend the evening star gazing. At that latitude the sun sets at 6 p.m. You can literally see it sinking into the horizon. Once the sun goes down it is pitch black, and the stars pop out. They look so bright you would think you could touch them. The tropical night sky is beautiful. It was quiet and peaceful. The time must have been 10.30 or 11 p.m., and we were really slowing down and ready to call it a day when we could hear some motorboats out on the ocean. They seemed to be going up and down the coast. I asked Iris what she thought it was.

She said that it must be fishermen out for some night fishing, dragging their nets as they motored up and down.

It must have been a big school of fish, I thought. Iris's explanation sounded plausible to me. A little while later we heard a putt, putt, puttering coming from the night sky. *Now what on earth is that?* I asked.

She said she thought it sounded like helicopters, and that the Air Force must be doing night exercises.

It all sounded very logical to me. The very next thing there was an awful lot of activity coming from the posh hotels down the beach. Then a jeep came rushing out and down the lane to the main road. Next, a car from our motel was rushing in the same direction. What a lot of activity after sitting there in the peaceful tranquil night. I turned to Iris and said that they all must have run out of bread or something and were rushing in to town to put it their order for the next day. We both had a good laugh, because there was no town nearby, just a few scattered villages and one police station for the whole area. The closest town was Trincomalli, and that was about 12 miles away.

At last the excitement of the last few days got the better of us and we could not keep up any longer. Once we hit the bed it was lights out. We were in the Land of Nod. The next morning Thaw was coming to take us on the rest of our journey. He arrived bright and early the next morning. I can never understand these people. They get up even before the crack of dawn. The sun rises at 6 a.m but these hardy folk rise at 5 a.m. He arrived just as we were about to have breakfast. As he sat down to join us, he asked if everything was all right. By the tone of his voice I thought, *What a funny thing to say.* Yes, we replied, we have had a wonderful time.

Before we could rattle on and tell him all the wonderful things we had seen and done he asked if we had a good night's sleep. Well, by the look on his face we thought we had better pay attention to what he had to say. Now apparently the noises we had heard the night before were not what we had thought. The boats were the Sri Lankan Navy, and the helicopters were the Air Force, and they were not on night exercises. *It was the real thing!* The Tamil Tigers, the rebel army in Jaffna, were waiting in the ditches on the side of the road waiting for an opportune time to attack the police station. This was the police station just two miles from where we were. The military got a tip and managed to thwart the attack. Iris and I were blissfully unaware of all the ruckus. Things were now back to normal, Thaw assured us. Well, as normal as can be expected under the circumstances. We were more than willing to believe what he said. Looking back I wondered what the people from the hotels thought that they could do, rushing about in the dead of night.

Not many years later this place was decimated by the civil war. Some years later I revisited my lovely Nilavili. What buildings were left standing were riddled with bullet holes. The two posh hotels were practically destroyed, and our little motel lay in wrack and ruins.

Oh, what will become of my little island paradise?

Jaffna

Thaw had arrived early, and was eager to set off on the rest of our journey. The driver was waiting, also a couple of men on motorbikes. Thaw explained that as they were going to the same place as us, we could travel together. Thaw, after all, was still on duty as the head of security for the Bank of Ceylon. This still did not ring any warning bells. Security!

We were going up the eastern coast of Sri Lanka toward Jaffna. I must say that this coast line is the most beautiful and unspoiled I had ever seen. The road curved inland for a while, not a soul to be seen. Then we headed back towards the sea. Here the road ran parallel to the ocean. The sand is white, not a hint of pollution. After being on the road for about three hours we stopped for lunch. There on this lovely expanse of white beach was a white-washed bungalow, or rest house. It was the only building in sight. It almost glowed it was so bright, with the sun shining on it. Thaw had booked earlier for them to have lunch prepared. They were ready to serve us lunch. Oh! How I wished that they could have delayed the food so that I could go on this beach, maybe sneak a dip in the water. This really was unspoilt and pristine. The only other things on the beach for about two miles were a couple of fishing boats. No people. The place was very sparsely furnished, but it was clean. The tables were covered with nice white cloths. The food we were served was, of course, rice and curry. Very, very, very, HOT curry. I had banana chaser to cool the mouth. Bananas usually do the trick, but boy, was this hot. It was like eating fire. How on earth can people get used to eating food so fiery hot? But they can, and eventually I did also.

As we drove off I looked at the scene, trying to let the sight sink into my memory. The long stretch of white beach and two lonely fishing boats pulled out of the water, not a man in sight. Their work for the day done. The feeling I had was that I would not come this way again. As we drove on it was getting greener, and more lush vegetation.

Thaw was constantly looking 'round and would complain if one of the motor bikes got either too far ahead or too far behind, saying they should stay closer together. I thought, *What difference does it make unless they didn't know the way and could get lost.* Iris and I were still oblivious. We were just enjoying the change of scenery. It never ceased to amaze me how it could be so different around the next bend. We drove close to the ocean for quite some time. We didn't see any people. The only thing to show that there were any people living there was a lonely fisherman's hut here and there on the beach.

Like I have said, I was so glad that we had a driver. The roads were in pretty bad shape, in need of many repairs. We came up to a river and had to wait on the river bank for the ferry on the other side of the river to fill up with passengers, then come over to our side of the river. We waited and waited. No one was in a hurry here. Eventually the ferry came, and people got off. Now we were cleared to get on. This was the strangest ferry I had ever seen. It didn't have a motor that I could see. It looked more like a flat-bed tugboat. The sides were very low. One false move, and you would be in the drink. We drove the car on and got out to stretch our legs. We had to be careful, as there was not a lot of room. There were only a couple of feet on either side of the car.

There was a thick rope from one side of the river bank to the other. I wondered what for. Once we were "all aboard" I soon found out. This rope was to pull the ferry across the river, and all were expected to do their share of pulling. So Thaw, Iris, and I did our share. As you would imagine, this brought a lot of grins from the locals. Here was this white woman in the faithful floppy red hat, pulling on a rope in order to get to the other side. A bit like, why did the chicken cross the road.... I felt like I was in a soap opera.

We had one more river to cross before we got to Thaw's destination. We were getting closer to Jaffna. As we came upon villages I was interested in how differently they lived. It seemed they really liked their privacy. Almost without exception each house had a high fence around it. And even more interestingly, it looked like they had cut branches off a tree or shrub, stuck them in the ground to form a fence. And these sticks were sprouting, growing leaves and taking root. There were some fences that had grown almost into hedges. I found later that this was quite common in this part of the country. You could stick anything into the ground, and it would grow, it was such a lush fertile land.

Finally we reached our cut-off road leading to the bank that Thaw was to visit. Five or so miles, and we were there. It was really just a hole in the wall, a little village with one or two homes. There were the bank and some little village huts, no shops or any amenities, and by this time I needed the amenities.

Thaw, the driver, and the two motorbikers went into the bank. Iris and I took a stroll around this little village. We walked along the road for about one mile, then turned round and walked back. That was enough to get the curious out to stare at us. There was nothing else for us to do but go back to the car. There we waited in the baking-hot car. It wasn't long before Thaw came out, and we were on our way, minus the two motorbikers. Thaw was visibly relieved as he got into the car, and we were now on our way again. Now was time for Thaw to reveal all. The two motorcyclists were, in fact, trained and armed security guards. Thaw had a revolver on the floor of the car at his feet. He said that the bank had asked him to transport money from Trincomali, a very large sum, 20 million rupees, in fact. Oh! Boy, were we glad that we knew nothing about it. To think that Iris and I were, in fact, like decoys. This was potentially very dangerous, particularly with the situation between the rebel Tigers and the Sri Lankan armed forces. If the rebels had got wind of it, it could have been very serious. I was very happy that I knew nothing of it. So was Iris. We began to unwind, as we were now on our return journey.

We were almost at the northern tip of the island of Sri Lanka. We were only about twenty-five miles from the place where the film, "Elephant walk," staring Elizabeth Taylor was filmed. If you get a chance to see this film you will see how the elephants make their seasonal migration, and nothing can stand in their way. Anyone who builds in their path should consider the consequences, just like the elephants at Iris and Thaw's home in Trincomali. All that said, we now had to return home. I was by now looking forward to getting back to my bungalow in Mount Lavinia.

We had had a wonderful vacation filled with sights and experiences that I would never have believed had I not been on that wonderful trip. I look back with fond memories of my lovely Sri Lanka, and to my two dear friends, Iris and Thaw.

The Funeral

Living in Sri Lanka certainly had its moments. Some rather extraordinary things can happen, like the time I had to perform a funeral at the last moment. This is how it all came about.

My husband's cousin, Erskin, who was 60 years old and had been a drinker most of those years, had recently married Yvonne, a young woman of about 28 years, who also liked to have a drink. I'm sure their union was by mutual agreement. She was quite an attractive young woman, and after hearing her story of abuse I could understand her turning to the numbing effect of drink. He, however, was a bit worse for the wear. They were drinking partners, so I suppose that was their main attraction. They came to visit me, and I found Yvonne a very nice young woman. She would visit from time to time, and was always on good behaviour. I liked her, and I guess she felt the same way about me. Now her husband Erskin was another story. He was a real con artist, a likable enough guy, but I was always wary of him, always on guard.

I was surprised one day when I got a message from Yvonne that she was in hospital. The hospital is a free hospital in Dehiwalla, a district of Colombo not too far from where I lived. So off I went to see her. When I got there I got the shock of my life. The hospital was comprised of several buildings, all bungalow style, built, I am sure by the British. I think they had seen better days. I asked the way from an orderly. He almost took me by the hand to show me the ward that she was in. I found in Sri Lanka that white people got preferential treatment. I went to her ward and was greeted by an awful sight. The buildings were very run down. On the outside they were a dirty grey colour, and had not seen a lick of paint for years, or as they say, since the Quakers walked to France.

In their defence I have to say that everything was difficult to get in Sri Lanka, and everything is at a premium. This is a third-world country, and paint was the last thing they spent their money on. Cleanliness, on the other hand, is cheap. The first thing that greeted me was the most awful smell. The ward that Yvonne was in was a large room with half walls, so you could see outside. It was a nice idea, really. It allowed the air to flow through. There was a corridor around three sides of the ward. This also had half walls. As I walked down the corridor there were women sitting or lying on wooden benches. Some were sitting on mats on the floor. All of them looked sick. I don't think anyone would want to be in there if she were not really very ill.

Once inside the ward proper I was amazed how close the beds were; there certainly was no room for privacy. Yvonne was very pleased to see me. She had been rushed in the day before and explained that when anyone comes to this hospital they have to bring their own bed linen or sleep on sheets from the previous patient. By the look of the sheets the person before must have died there. The sheets were blood stained and dirty looking. Because Yvonne had been rushed in she did not have clean sheets. We visited for a while, I said my good byes, and promised to return before the evening with clean sheets. True to my word I returned in the evening with whatever toiletries I thought she needed, along with the sheets.

Now by the time I got there visiting was over, and they were not going to allow me in. But being the kind of person that I am, and being white I wheedled my way in. When I was walking along the corridor I was shocked to see all the women that I had seen earlier in the day still there. Now I realised that this was over crowding to the extreme. As quickly as possible I changed Yvonne's bed covers. I was ready to say my goodbye when we both got the most awful smell, a really bad, foul odour. I thought I would throw up, so I left and said I would see her the next day. I was sorry to leave her there but could do nothing else.

The following day I planned my visit to coincide with the doctor's rounds. Boy, what a toffee-nosed snob this doctor was. She would never be a doctor in the West without a radical change of attitude. I have since realized that the feeling is that if you are an alcoholic then you deserve what you get. Also, the poor and needy get no respect from this kind of doctor. The rich think that they have special privileges. I have seen the wealthy treat their servants shamefully. I found out later that Yvonne's condition was very serious. As I was about to leave Yvonne whispered, "You know that smell last night? Well, a dog wandered into the ladies shower room and died. It was only discovered when the cleaners came in the morning." That just made me sick to my stomach.

A couple of days later she was allowed to leave, provided she had someone to care for her. So she came to stay with me for a while. I got in touch with her family doctor. She came and visited whenever needed. She was a very caring person, but she gave me the sense that Yvonne would get better. I was under the impression that if we did every thing she suggested then she would recover. Yvonne came to church with me, gave her heart to Jesus, saying she wished her sister; father and uncle would do the same. She finally did find peace; however, she still had the yearning for liquor. She would try to get drinks all over the place, even asking my housekeeper to get her some. She gradually got worse. I then got the name of another doctor, a specialist with a good reputation as the best in town. We went to see him, even though people said without an appointment we would not get to see him, as he was a very important man in his field. I figured the colour of my skin might help us get in to see him.

This man was quite different from the other doctors we had seen. When he came to call the next patient he took one look at Yvonne and called her and me into his office instead. He gave her a thorough examination. The doctor in the hospital didn't even want to touch her. This doctor was a lot more caring and compassionate and said that she should be admitted to hospital at once. Then he asked her to wait in the waiting room while he made the arrangements with me. He then told me that she was very ill and would not live more than a few weeks. I was dumfounded; I had thought there was a chance of recovery.

Arrangements were made, and I got directions to the Jayawardener Hospital. She and I drove straight there. All the time I was conscious of not letting her see how upset I was. I was armed with a letter from the doctor and a hospital pass. This hospital is way out in the country. It was a brand-new facility built by the Japanese. I was very impressed. It is a three-or-four-storied building. Her ward was on the top floor. This hospital had the same basic layout as the other hospital with the half walls, making it nice and airy. The big differences were that it was brand new, clean, and bright. I was not allowed to stay any length of time, just long enough for her to be admitted. Even the nurses were pleasant and smiling. I went back one more time to see her. The open ward gave a view of the surrounding countryside; it was pretty with all the lush greenery. This was the perfect place to be if you were sick. She was happy there; the nurses treated her like she was their little sister. A few days later she was released from there and went to stay with her father and uncle, who lived just a few streets away from my home. I went to see her there and wondered how they all managed. It was such a tiny place, not really big enough for one person, let alone three. It was quite understandable that she wanted to be with her family. She came to see me a couple of days later. She looked really well.

So well, in fact, that I thought there was at least a possibility that she would recover. I really prayed that she would. She said that she was very tired. I thought that was a result of the unusual activity of walking to my house. I just prayed that she would not give up hope. It is such a shame for someone so young to go through this kind of things she had endured. A day or two later she went to visit her husband, and while there, she passed away. I drove Erskin to the hospital to deal with the documentation, because she had died at home. Then I stepped aside and let the family take over. I got all the information about the funeral. It was to be held at Erskin's mother's house. They still do things like they did in the bygone years; the body was laid out at home so that friends and family could pay their last respects. She was laid out in an open coffin in the living room. Now not being one of the immediate family I stayed away until the day of the funeral. I just attended to show my last respects to Yvonne and her family. Later that day her sister came to my home. She was in a very distressed state. Yvonne, her elder sister, was dead at such very young age. She was also concerned because Erskin wanted to put Yvonne in one of his mother's red velvet dresses. This was not at all appropriate for a young women. Erskin's mother, Aunty Violet, was at least 80 years old. She asked me, "Aunty, can't you do something about it?"

Well, as much as I would have liked to help there was nothing I could do. I could pray and that's what I did.

The morning of the funeral arrived, and as is custom, they had erected an awning in the front garden with metal chairs. These chairs can get pretty hot, even in the shade. I went along with Blossom, another of my husband's cousins. She is a Christian also. We arrived and sat out on the hot chairs. We waited and waited for the ceremony to get started, and we waited, and waited. Each moment we were getting hotter. Now they do things quite differently to what I am used to. The Catholic priest was to come to the house and do the Catholic service.

Then everyone would go to the cemetery, and there the Anglican priest would do the Anglican ceremony for the interment. Well, like I said, we were still waiting when a man came out and told Blossom and me that the Catholic priest was not going to come. He told us that the evening before the priest had come to give his sympathy and to make all the usual arrangements for the following day. Well, Erskin was, as usual, as drunk as a fiddler's bitch. He had picked up their little pooch and held it over the coffin to say goodbye to Yvonne. Like I say he was as drunk as a skunk, and he dropped the dog into the coffin on top of the body. The priest was disgusted at Erskin's drunken state and, said he was so shocked and disgusted that he would not come the following day to do the service. Erskin had not taken him seriously or had been too drunk to understand and had not made alternate arrangements.

Here was this man with a pleading face, shaking his head, saying to Blossom and me, "Aye oh, Shame. No, aunty, ah nay, what to do? No." Then he dropped a real clanger and looking at me said, "Won't you do the service, Aunty?"

My mouth fell open, and my eyes nearly fell out of my head. *What me? Oh, no!* I turned to Blossom and said, "You're local; you can do it." I thought she was going to get up and run; she was even more scared than me.

The man went inside again. And once again we waited. Then after a while he came back out again and gave me that look, with his head to one side, not just a pleading look but a *pleading, pleading,* look. Now I thought that if we stayed outside any longer we would all be fainting from the heat. So I took the bull by the horns said a quick prayer. I asked the Lord to help so that I would do Yvonne justice. Give her a good send off, so to speak. She had not had a good life; the least we could do was give her an appropriate service. I went into the house, which was even more crowded than the garden, and of course it was hotter and steamier. I thought I had better carry my Bible, look as if I knew what I was doing.

I stood at the head of the coffin. How did I know it was the head of the coffin? *WELL*, there was the head. Did I mention that it was an *open* coffin? I don't think I ever saw a dead body before this. The body was not embalmed, so we had to get moving. The heat was having its effect on the corpse. It was beginning to have a distinct odour. I can't remember exactly what I said, but I did say what a loving person Yvonne had been and that she would be dearly missed. I said how she had made her peace with the Lord, and what a comfort it had been to her in the last weeks of her life. She had told me that she wished that her sister, father, uncle, and husband would find the love and joy that she had in her saviour, Jesus.

I figured that I had said enough when someone handed me a hymn sheet. Hint. Hint. I started to lead the mourners in one of the usual funeral hymns. Now you have to understand, I have a very deep voice. I have been told that I sing alto. I think it is more like scraping the bottom of a barrel. At the church I attended in Montreal I was asked if I would like to join the choir, as they needed more male voices. The folks tried to sing along with me, but were unable to keep the tune. Then a lovely Catholic lady stood next to me, and in her beautiful soprano voice took over. I stepped back and let the others take over from there.

The rest of the service I do not remember. I have racked my brain, but it is no good. I do not remember going to the cemetery, and I am sure that I did. One thing I do know is that Blossom was glad that I did the honours, and she did not have to. The amazing thing is they think if you have a fair skin and come from the west you have more authority. We all know that is not so. I'm sure after the service others must have thought, *I could have done that.* It was a sad ending to such a young life, but there is comfort in knowing she is at peace at last with her Lord Jesus Christ. I heard from Blossom only a year or two ago that Erskin had also passed on. How wonderful that before he died he had made his peace with his Lord Jesus. God does answer prayers.

The Money Exchangers

I had been living in Sri Lanka for five years. My husband and I had moved to his place of birth expecting to live out the rest of our lives on this beautiful Island. Unfortunately, we found out that he had lung cancer after being here only a few months. By the end of the year he had passed away. Now after four years on my own I decided that I should return to Canada and be closer to my sons.

I had made many friends while here. Some of my friends were also foreigners from all over the globe. They came from Germany, Holland, and Australia. One by one they all left Sri Lanka. Even though I had many dear local friends I still felt vulnerable, especially with the volatile situation in the country. Some of the things happening there were very scary.

There were the two elderly sisters who lived down the street from me. One of them was an avid cricket fan. She went to a neighbor's home to watch it on the TV While she was out someone came in the house to rob whatever they could, and finding her sister there alone they killed her.

Then there was the time when my housekeeper arrived late for work. She was all excited and shaking. The reason she gave was that as she was walking down the road she saw a crowd. People were shouting and waving their arms about. So she went to see what all the excitement was. Well, it appeared that there had been a gang killing in the early morning. A man had been murdered and chopped up. His body was strewn all over the street. Of course she had to give me all the gory details. His torso was on this side of the street his head in the gutter on the other side of the street. His arms and legs were half a mile down the road. The theory was that body parts had been tossed from a moving vehicle. This had all happened within half a mile of my home.

I was always on guard, as men would constantly be trying to climb the parapet wall around my home. The only reason I could think of was that they intended to rob me. I found that the best defense was to raise my voice, thus alerting the neighbors. This way the person would be seen and recognized. Now I think back, if they had been rebels my shouting would not have made a bit of difference.

Well, all of this really prompted me to sell my beautiful home. I loved this house. It was quiet and peaceful. I would sit in the living room in the early morning or late afternoon, the warm sea breeze blowing on the white curtains, causing them to billow like white clouds. I have many memories of this place, some of them quite unusual.

Like the time I was giving my house a spring cleaning. I was polishing the floor when I saw some black ants creeping out of the door frame. Now the door frame was built of hard wood that must have been 8 inches by 8 inches, and very dense. I thought I would make short work of them, so I got out the Baygon. This is a bug and mosquito spray that really knocks them dead. Actually I would spray the whole house about twice a day to keep the mosquitoes away.

I found the little hole where the ants were coming out, gave a couple of good squirts, then I went about my work. After about fifteen minuets I turned around and got the shock of my life. There, marching across my freshly polished floor, were literally thousands of black ants. I was running about like a lunatic spraying, saying, "Oh, my goodness! Oh, my goodness!" That spray should have been enough, or so I thought. I swept the ants of the floor and out the door. I felt quite sorry, because as I swept them out the birds came swooping down to eat them up. Poor birds. I bet they didn't last long with all that Baygon inside them. There was nothing I could do, so I went into the kitchen to start my cooking, quite confident that the ants had breathed their last breath. I went into the living room some time later. What a shock I got!

There were millions and millions, well, that's what it seemed like to me, of ants marching across the floor. Once again out came the broom. I swept them out the door; again the birds swoop down for the feed. Again I got out the Baygon. This time I aimed the nozzle right into the hole. That did it; great big clumps of ants fell out of the door frame. It was a good job the wood was so thick; otherwise the strength of the frame would have been compromised. Things like this were, believe it or not, quite the norm in this country

Then there was the time when I found a snake in the laundry room. It was a large one, about five feet long. What I was more worried about was if it was poisonous or not. There were some men working on a house down the lane, so I went and asked them if they could help me. "Oh, yes, madam," they said until I told them about the snake Then they were suddenly too busy to help me.

I had to think fast, as I still had a snake in my laundry room. So I said, "Three strong men like you, and you can't help a poor white women like me?"

That did it, at least saying they were strong men may have tipped the scales in my favor. They came to my house armed with shovels and brooms. When they saw the size of the snake they almost lost their courage. I asked them if it was a poisonous one. They said it was a rat snake and not poisonous. So we four, armed with sticks, a broom, and a shovel, poked and prodded and swept the snake out of the room and into the drainage ditch. As they did it I could see they were quite pleased with themselves. They would have a story to tell once they got home. I'm sure each would tell it with him as the hero.

Well, all these things spooked me out. That is why I decided to leave the island. I liquidated all my assets. I was fortunate to sell the house, being paid in Cooks travelers checks.

The car, however, was a different story. I had 400,000 rupees that had to be converted into dollars. Now the banks could not do this, something to do with taking money out of the country. In other words, it was illegal to do so.

Well, illegal or not, I had to transfer this money into dollars. I was not intending to return any time soon, and rupees were no good to me in Canada. My friends Blossom and Surani said, "Oh, not to worry, Maureen; there are money changers in the fort." Now the fort was the financial area of the city but you wouldn't know it to look at it. It was a hodgepodge of high-rise office buildings and pokey little stores that to me seemed dark and devious, which I suppose in reality was just what they were. Now I was expecting a small office with at least the appearance of a financial institution.

We drove into town and parked the car at the Intercontinental Hotel. We had to walk across the busy street and down the block, all the time being pestered by hawkers and being bumped this way and that. One time I had been walking down this road when two men tried to rob the watch right off my arm, so I was apprehensive, to say the least. Remember, I had 400,000 rupees in my handbag that was, by the way, tucked tightly under my arm. I was trying to look as relaxed as I could.

Surani and Blossom led me into this little shop. It was all of ten feet square and looked like it had not seen a lick of paint since colonial days. There was a counter across the room, and behind it sat a rather large, oily, and sullen man. He had hardly any room to turn around. In front of the counter there was just enough room for three rickety wooden chairs. I was thankful that there were only three; then no one could sit next to me. This was like a scene out of one of Charles Dickens' novels, and I was very uptight.

I think the man could only talk in one-word sentences. He barely looked at me, and in a gruff, gangster-like voice (well I thought that's what he sounded like), he asked, "What?"

I told him that I wanted to change rupees into dollars.

He asked, "how much?"

Now I was really nervous to tell him how much. This was a lot of money for me. I can look back and see that to him it was a pittance. But you wouldn't think so by his appearance; his clothes were not too clean. Neither was his smell. He looked like a Tamil, and they have the habit of rubbing their bodies with ginger oil. It is supposed to make them healthy and strong. Well, he was strong all right, strong smelling from the ginger oil. Not saying another word he just held his hand out for my money, and like a meek little lamb I handed over this small fortune.

He took it without another word and stuffed it into a drawer at his belly. Anyone wanting to rob him would have to get past that mound. He said, "Sit."

I did as I was told, sitting in the only vacant chair next to Surani. Now I thought that Surani and Blossom were there to give me moral support. But while this transaction was going on I could hear them talking away, saying, "You know so and so; well, you never know what she said...Blah, Blah, Blah," while I was wringing my hands. Well, not in reality, but inside I was wringing my hands.

In came a scrawny young man. His countenance was like the large man behind the counter. I wondered if this was a job requirement. The large man muttered something to the young man, then handed him some of my money. With that the young man was off out the door. I thought, *That's it; I'm done for.* Then I waited and waited, wondering if there was any point, if my money was gone. I wanted to turn to my support couple, but they were now talking about this lady who sang too loud in church. What a showoff, and she didn't have such a good voice anyway. So I kept quiet, my stomach in knots.

The young scrawny man came back, handed the large man some money, which he quickly stuffed inside the drawer. He handed some more money over with whispered instructions, and the young one was gone again. This happened several more times.

Eventually the large man crooked his finger at me, and in a gruff voice said, "Come." He sat there and counted out American dollars onto the counter and pushed them over to me. Now I didn't count out the money with him, and I wasn't about to recount it in the store. I just grabbed it and stuffed it into my handbag. Now I had to walk down the street across the road with these two chatter boxes, with everyone knowing I just came out of the money-changer's shop. I'm sure that not everyone knew, but you never know, do you? Phew! I could only breathe a sigh of relief when I was in the car and on the way home. My flight out of the country was in one week, and I could only pray that no one would find out that I had that much money in the house. My mind was playing tricks on me. Could I end up like the body cut up and strewn all over the road?

Leaving the country with all that money was my next hurdle. I had the traveler's checks plus the cash from the sale of the car. The man who bought my house was a customs agent at the airport. He said he would be there at the time of my flight, and if there was any problem he would step in.

I did not know this man at all except he bought my house. He also gyped me at the last moment by reducing the payment on the house by quite a large amount. He had me over a barrel. What could I do? I was all ready to move. So he was not that honorable, and I wondered how much I could trust him. Well, I got to the airport on the day of departure, trying to look calm and collected, when really I was a mess inside. There was an elderly German lady, and she was in a state because there was a departure tax to be paid on leaving the country. She was saying, "Why didn't someone tell me? I have no money! I gave it all away before leaving the hotel!"

It was a very small amount, but they were not going to let her leave without paying her 25 rupees. I didn't want to draw attention to myself, but on the other hand, how could I see her so distraught? So I paid the tax for her. As you can imagine she was really relived.

I was feeling like I needed to pamper myself, so when I got to the ticket counter I asked if I could be bumped up to first class. They had room, so for $100 I traveled home in comfort. I sat in the comfortable first-class seats and put my feet up.

As the plane took off I looked out the window at my adopted land. I was leaving my beautiful island, Sri Lanka for the very last time. I have not returned not even for a visit. At least I still have my memories. No one can take them away, and I still live in the hopes of returning some day.

Also available from PublishAmerica

BEHIND THE SHADOWS
by Susan C. Finelli

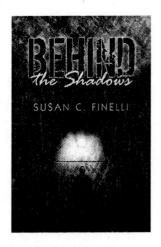

Born into squalor, Raymond Nasco's quest
for wealth and power shrouds two
generations with deceit, murder, rape and illicit
love. Setting his sights above and beyond
the family's two-room apartment in a New
York City lower eastside tenement, Raymond
befriends Guy Straga, the son of a wealthy
business tycoon, and they develop a lifelong
friendship and bond. Caught in Raymond's
powerful grip, his wife, Adele, commits the
ultimate sin; and his son, Spencer, betrays
himself and the woman he loves and finally
becomes his father's son. Years later Kay
Straga stumbles upon the secret that has been
lurking in the shadows of the Straga and
Nasco families for two generations, a secret
that tempts her with forbidden love, a secret
that once uncovered will keep her in its
clutches from which there is no escape.

Paperback, 292 pages
6" x 9"
ISBN 1-4241-8974-8

About the author:

Susan C. Finelli has lived in New York all of her life and
has been a Manhattanite for over thirty years. She, her
husband John, and Riley Rian, their beloved cavalier
King Charles spaniel, currently reside in Manhattan,
and together they enjoy exploring the sights, sounds
and vibrancy of the Big Apple.

Available to all bookstores nationwide.
www.publishamerica.com